Frank Seaver is one of the last of the old time gunfighters, a man determined to put his past behind him and start all over again.

But life rarely offers second chances and after a fatal shooting in Missouri, Seaver finds himself on the run once again, pursued across a western frontier that grows more "civilized" every day. Once he reaches Montana, however, he becomes involved with the hunt for a savage cougar terrorizing the Yellowstone region. Seaver's interest in the expedition may have something to do with the attraction he feels for the lovely, long-suffering wife of the party's leader, world famous big game hunter, Philip Waring.

As the group makes its way through the stunning, mountainous landscape, personal conflicts and jealousies create dangerous divisions and rivalries, even as they prepare for a final, climactic confrontation with their deadly quarry...

I0677602

ALSO BY CLIFF BURNS

NOVELS
So Dark the Night
Of the Night

NOVELLAS
Righteous Blood

SHORT STORIES
The Reality Machine
Sex & Other Acts of the Imagination

THE LAST HUNT

A Novel of the Old West

Cliff Burns

Cover artwork: "The Warning Shadow" by William Robinson Leigh
(Courtesy the Rockwell Museum of Western Art; Corning, New York)

Cover design: Chris Kent

Interior design by Scribe Freelance | www.scribefreelance.com

Printed by: Lightning Source

Published by Black Dog Press (blackdogpress@yahoo.ca)

Author's website: http://cliffjburns.wordpress.com

ISBN: 978-0-9694853-5-3

for Ken Harman & "the cowboy way"

"The broadest truth about these strange, violent figures is that even well before the turn of the century they had been isolated as anarchic men of action in a nation slowly but steadily moving toward regimentation in lawful and orderly communities."

—JAMES D. HORAN,
The Gunfighters: The Authentic Wild West
(Crown Publishers; 1976)

"He did not need to tell anyone he was a bad one, for hell was written all over his face."

—ANDREW GARCIA,
Tough Trip Through Paradise (1878-79)
(Edited by Bennett H. Stein;
University of Idaho Press; 1967)

PROLOGUE

(Summer, 1884)

LONG BEFORE ACTUALLY setting eyes on Montana, Frank Seaver *dreamed* about it.

Bundled up in his bedroll somewhere in eastern Nebraska or shivering next to the fire in the foothills of the Rockies, an oilcloth spread beneath him to keep the damp out. Dozing off under a canopy of flickering stars and suddenly finding himself treated to panoramic views of snow-capped mountains, impenetrable forests and great expanses of sky arching toward far off horizons...

He blamed old Titus. The two of them crossed paths a few days after the trouble in St. Joe. Seaver had just started supper when someone "Hallo'd" his camp. He was on edge, expecting a posse, his response appropriately wary. But the elderly prospector soon put him at ease. Clearly he wasn't after anything except a little company and on close examination turned out to be as harmless (and chatty) as a jay.

Titus O'Rourke. "Of the County Antrim O'Rourkes and proud of it!" Short, bent with age and infirmity, blind in one eye, topped by a mane of white hair. A real character. Vigorously pumping Seaver's hand, his good eye fixed on the bubbling frying pan, assaying the fare. Seaver took pity on him, invited him to stay awhile, pouring his visitor a strong cup of *Arbuckle's* finest just to prove he was sincere.

O'Rourke was effusive in his thanks and spent the next two hours regaling him with tales of his journeys and adventures. If his meandering account was even halfway accurate, he'd racked up more travel miles than Marco Polo. He'd trekked through the entire west, from the gold fields of California to the remotest windblown butte in the Dakota Territory. Often alone and without a map, only the sun and stars to guide him. Quick wits and Irish luck had saved him more times than he could count. He'd wintered with the Shoshone, gone on war parties with the Crow and was blood brother to Crazy Horse.

Like most Irishmen, he told a good story. He became even more loquacious after digging out a bottle of "tarantula juice" and commenced taking long pulls on it at regular intervals.

"I tell you, son," O'Rourke belched dyspeptically, barely missing a beat, "this world is plumb full of marvels. I seen things you wouldn't hardly credit. Why, once up in Montana—"

Seaver spoke quietly from the other side of the fire. "Montana? I was ponderin' headin' that way myself."

Well, wouldn't you know it, it turned out that Montana was O'Rourke's favorite spot in the known world. He went on and on, waxing eloquent about the tall, reaching mountains and clear-running streams, wide open spaces and wildlife aplenty. Truly a Garden of Eden. "There are places and beasts in them parts no white man has set eyes on. You may think I'm repayin' your good company with nothin' but tall tales but believe me, God still has plenty o' mysteries to show us 'fore He's done."

It all sounded ideal to Seaver. He needed to lose himself, find somewhere far off where he could start fresh, with a clean slate. He plied O'Rourke with questions and the two of them ended up conversing well into the night.

The next morning, Titus, feeling the effects of the rotgut whiskey, wasn't nearly as forthcoming. They shared a cup of coffee together before parting company, Titus heading east, Seaver steering northwest, intending to follow the Platte as far as it took him. When crossing the plains, numberless miles of desolate prairie, it wasn't prudent to ignore a known water source, even one rumored to be *too thick to drink and too thin to plow.*

As they took leave of each other, Titus gave him a bleary once over. "Don't believe I caught your name, stranger."

"Thornton. Frank Thornton." The lie came easily, Thornton was his mother's maiden name.

He would be "Frank Thornton" from now on and that night he made it official, shaving off the thick, drooping moustache he'd cultivated since his early twenties. A trademark and distinguishing feature that was bound to figure prominently on circulars so off it went. His bare lip felt unnatural, naked. He was glad no one was around to see it.

It was time to take stock. He had a good mount and packhorse, both of which he could exchange or replace as the need arose. He was well provisioned for a long journey, with no attachments holding him back. A man of independent means. Nothing to keep him from going where he pleased and doing what he liked.

Nothing except he was wanted by the law, a violent, dangerous desperado who had committed a capital crime.

Shaving off his moustache wasn't going to be enough. The transformation had to be complete. He shucked his fancy threads, the frock coat and tailored breeches, changed into saddleworn Levis, a long-sleeved cotton shirt, leather vest. Dispensed with the felt slouch hat, replacing it with a sun-bleached Stetson.

Parting with his faithful Colt .45 was hard. He felt

incomplete without it. But it was a relic of another time, another man. He replaced it with a .44 Remington, a gun acquired during his days as a lawman, dependable, with a reassuring heft.

It was important to present a low profile. Leave a cold trail for potential pursuers. He resolved to stay away from towns and settlements, avoid people, but that wasn't easy, even for a naturally solitary man. Ten days in the saddle with no company but crickets and prairie dogs wore on a person.

In his younger days, employed as a line rider, he could go a month, sometimes longer, never seeing another human face. Now he was older and it was different. Being alone all the time was hard, hard on the *spirit*. It got so you wondered if anyone even knew or cared you were alive. A bad feeling and one not easily shaken off.

Western Nebraska, two weeks later:
Seaver used the excuse that he was low on salt to stop at the next homestead he encountered. Which turned out to be a beaten down shack a few hundred yards from the banks of the North Platte. There was nothin' but *nothin'* in every direction, as his daddy used to say. No neighbors, no other living creatures in sight except birds on the wing.

Her name was Jenny Udall and she was, he quickly determined, a grass widow. Her husband Warren either dead or just plain *gone*, she wasn't sure which.

"Ain't seen him since spring. Lit out from here, never said where he was goin' or if he was comin' back." She seemed resigned to her situation, the hard hand she'd been dealt. She said she was twenty-five but looked ten years older. No crops had been planted and her larder was nearly empty. There were grim days ahead.

He ended up scouring the countryside for firewood, filling in the chinks in her walls with straw and mud, patching her leaky roof. The hunting was poor but he did his best. It turned out she was a good cook and her company agreeable but after three days of it he was uneasy. Frequently glancing over his shoulder, scanning the eastern skyline.

One night, in the pale, smoky light cast by an improvised Betty lamp, he saw the way she was looking at him, the intensity of her gaze. It unsettled him, the *need* he detected there.

He left at daybreak. Exchanged but a perfunctory word or two with her before swinging up onto his saddle and hightailing it out of there. Knowing he would remember the look on her face for as long as he lived.

Someone else was bound to come along. Surely.

A bigger, better man who could endure what the place would demand of him. The loneliness, most of all. No friends, no diversions, nearest neighbor ten miles away. Eagerly anticipating the twice-yearly trips to town for provisions, a chance to converse with other human beings, catch up on the latest news. Breaking his back plowing a hundred and sixty stony acres, hand-seeding it with Turkey Red Wheat...and then watching helplessly as every stalk of it was devoured by drought, insects or an early frost.

No wonder Udall skedaddled. If his wife had any sense, she'd do the same.

Thereafter he kept to himself, made do with less salt.

Shaking the Nebraska dust from his clothes and just keeping on keeping on. He knew he was in the Wyoming Territory because the elevation was rising, the nights colder. Enjoying a good fire, not hiding his presence but not advertising it either. He liked to leave enough time so he had an hour of light to read by. Sometimes, if the book was especially good, he burned a candle. He was partial to Dickens and Shakespeare. He couldn't recall once shedding a tear for any of the things he'd done, but sometimes, as he read a particularly beautiful passage, he was moved, overcome by emotions he never knew he possessed.

He slept with a Winchester rifle beside him and the Remington stashed under his roll. He was a light sleeper and the hard ground and primitive conditions didn't help any. Part of him nostalgic for a warm feather bed and nickel beer. Definitely feeling the chill more than he used to; it seeped deep into his bones, leaving a residual ache that set his teeth on edge.

He banked up the fire, made sure there was wood for morning. Then he smiled, thinking about Titus, wondering where the old boy might be resting his head at that moment. Suddenly experiencing a profound sense of futility and despair, the universe immense and indifferent above him, his existence pathetic and inconsequential in comparison. Never had he felt more isolated and alone.

But he wasn't really alone, was he? Somewhere out there, who knew how far away, his pursuers had also bedded down for the night and were regarding the same sky he was. Men with vengeful hearts, selected for their proficiency with weapons and propensity for violence. Deputized in haste, perhaps as much a lynch party as a posse.

He slipped his book, Voltaire's *Candide,* into a leather pouch he'd purchased from an old woman in Nacogdoches. A weathered, dignified face, those dark, Mexican eyes. The satchel hand-made, skillfully wrought. It had preserved many a volume from wind, rain and desert heat. The pouch went into the same saddlebag as the Colt. Each possessing its own intrinsic value.

He checked the rifle, then settled down to sleep. It was a still night and for once the bugs were downright tolerable.

Montana, meanwhile, was getting closer every day. He could tell because his dreams were becoming more and more vivid. Overflowing with remarkable detail. He saw wildlife, bears and deer and elk. Existing in an unspoiled environment, no signs of men or civilization, as pristine as it was on the First Day.

But even in his dreams, he knew it wouldn't last...

CHAPTER ONE

CHEYENNE WAS TEMPTING. He had no history there and debated making an exploratory visit. Seaver got close enough to see some of its outlying buildings and hear the distant bawling of cattle milling about in the city's extensive stockyards. Cheyenne, after all, owed its existence to the railroad and the famous Goodnight-Loving Trail, which ferried countless head up from Texas for shipping to points east and west.

It was a bustling, prosperous city, tree-lined streets, fancy hotels and more lawyers than you could shoot. A thoroughly *civilized* place, thousands of people living in close quarters, bumping elbows and still remaining civil, instead of slapping for their guns at the slightest affront.

He had shaved off his mustache, allowed his sideburns to grow. Different clothes and a different man. He could almost pass for normal.

At some point the Thornton persona he'd adopted would have to be introduced to the rest of the world. But not in Cheyenne. Too many people and lawmen aplenty. The telegraph always racing ahead, tapping out its bad news. Followed by handbills, crudely drawn and promising lavish rewards: dead or alive.

My name is Frank Thornton. Thornton's the name. How d'you do, ma'am? Frank Thornton. Frank Thornton, at your service.

He continued north, the altitude thinning the air. Some mornings he woke with frost on his bedding, his breath visible in the early light.

His mount developed a wheeze and neither horse inspired much confidence for the long haul. Luckily, he was passing by Fort Fetterman and while the army might have pulled up stakes, a settlement, of sorts, remained. He could buy provisions, hopefully replace the horses, walk around, stretch some of the ache out of his knees.

The place wasn't much to look at, two years abandoned and already falling into disrepair. Some of the outbuildings stripped or carted off. The wooden walls still stood, a score or so tents and tepees erected nearby. There was a heavy gate that could be swung closed at night but mostly they didn't bother. Conditions were primitive and the patrons on the rough side. He knew they were eyeballing him, sizing him up. He stepped aside for no one, staring right back at them.

There were no takers. Something in his face forbade disagreement and no man among them, white or red, seemed inclined to give him quarrel or complaint.

He spotted some sporting women but put such notions out of his mind. Or tried to. It had been awhile. He frequented all three saloons, two of which were housed in pavilion tents dating back to the Civil War. Gathered whatever gossip and information he could (usually more of the former than the latter).

At one establishment, cleverly dubbed "Fetterman's Revenge", he insinuated himself into a group observing a friendly poker game. Most of the players were familiar with each other and kept up a lively banter, regularly infused with personal invective and cuss words. One of them was the local dentist, Doc Throckmorton, and he provided the most interesting tidbits, information literally pried from some of his recent patients.

"Have ye heard the latest about that big cat? Dang you,

Herbert," he complained to the corpulent dealer, "don't them fat fingers of yours ever grace a fellow with the card he requires?" He stuck a pipe between his lips, bit down on the stem. "Like I says, have y'all heard about that killer cat they been talkin' about?"

"Do tell," the man on his left spoke up companionably. He was holding three jacks and sitting pretty.

"Yeah," Burt, the dentist's *bête noir* across the table quipped, "let's hear some more o' your lies. How big is your cat this time round? Last I heard it could swallow up three men at once and come back for seconds."

Throckmorton endured the joshing with good humor. "Well, think what ye like but this fella told me it's already kilt five men and that's jes' the ones they know of." He mopped his sweaty brow with a dirty handkerchief. "Sounds to me like it has acquired an appetite for human flesh."

"I hear the thing's unnatural," a cowboy next to Seaver blurted out. He was missing the top half of one ear and dustier than the Sahara Desert. "Something spawned down below." Snickers greeted the remark. This wasn't a crowd of good, God-fearing Baptists.

"That's foolish speculation," Doc Throckmorton demurred. "This creature is some kind of remnant from our prehistoric past. A freak of nature and undoubtedly one of a kind. A rare animal...and it'll take a rare man to bring it down."

Seaver was intrigued. "Where'd you say this cat is supposed to be at?"

Doc took out his pipe, scratched his nose with it. "Over yonder in the Yellowstone. They made it a park a few years back. And I hear it's the most wondrous spot on God's green world..."

Later, Seaver paid a visit to the livery stable to see what

was available. It consisted of a dilapidated barn and circular corral, all of it held together by spit and a prayer. The pickings were slim—scrubs, mostly, but then he caught sight of a fine-looking animal hobbled and close-tied to a snubbing post at the far end of the corral. The handsome sorrel was clearly the best of the lot, but when he inquired about its peculiar circumstances, Ed Weight, the proprietor, almost swallowed an entire plug of tobacco.

"Forget it. That critter is horsemeat, soon as I get 'round to it." He waved a bandaged hand at Seaver. "Lookit! Took a chunk out o' me the size of an egg. I'm gonna shoot that no-good, goddamn nag...but first I'm gonna let it suffer awhile." Nodding in satisfaction. "Ain't had no food or water since yesterday and I got it rigged so it can't even twitch a muscle. Give it a lick or two with *this* when it suits me too." Brandishing a quirt of plaited leather. A vicious, stupid man. Filthy bib overalls and the yellowest eyes Seaver had ever seen. Wolf eyes.

"Layin' it on a bit thick, ain't you?"

"Mister, you don't know the half of it." He jerked a thumb toward the corral. "Thing's loco. Kicked the hell out of its stall, jes' about kills any horse that goes near it. Every so often you come across one that's jes' plain *bad*. Can't be cured, can't be helped. Best to shoot 'em, skin 'em and leave the rest to the buzzards."

"I'll give you thirty silver dollars for him."

"Huh?" Weight stared at him. "Ain't you heard anything I—"

"Thirty dollars and I ride him out of here." Weight gaped at him as he counted out the money.

"Fair warnin', mister." Weight pocketed the currency with undisguised glee. "That critter been gelded but it sure as hell ain't been gentled."

"I understand." Turning to gaze at his latest acquisition. "My daddy always told me to avoid yellow-haired women and horses with more spirit than sense." Taking a deep breath. "He was right about the women. Guess I'm about to find out what kind of judge of horse flesh he was."

The big gelding was tall, thin-necked. Wide-bodied, he liked that, fifteen, maybe sixteen hands. A striking russet color, black mane and tail. *Beautiful.*

It appeared to take no notice as he approached with his saddle and gear. He loosened the tether so it could raise its head, stand comfortably. This close, he could fully appreciate what a superb animal it was: well-proportioned, every ripple of muscle revealing its breeding and quality.

He maintained eye contact, always staying where it could see him. Talking, keeping his voice low and monotonous. Using the Spanish phrases Hector had taught him almost two decades ago.

"*Ven, mi belleza...*"

Hector believed most of the horses in the New World originated from Spanish stock, animals brought over by Cortez and his bunch. Somehow or other, horses still retained some understanding or memory of their old *conquistador* masters. *Speak to them in the mother tongue,* Hector instructed him, *talk to them until part of them remembers...and obeys.*

Hector was a wise old hand who knew a thing or two about horses. Didn't hoard his knowledge like some of the others did and Seaver spent many long hours learning the cowboy way at the feet of a master.

Now he was putting some of that wisdom to good use, cooing to the sorrel, using phrases he didn't entirely understand but which Hector assured him would tame the orneriest broncos and bring them to heel.

"Calma...calma...mantenga la calma, mi hermosa..."

He kept talking, holding the animal's gaze. Stroking its neck, moving in closer, letting it smell him. He saw spirit and intelligence in its brown eyes, wariness too. "I been so low, I was down to boots and saddle. Tough times. But I'd never stoop so low that I'd raise a hand against the likes of you. I admire your proud heart." Vowing: "I'll be the last one that ever rides you. No other man will claim that right."

The horse shied away some as he swung first a blanket, then the forty-pound saddle onto its back, but the restraints kept it from bolting. He noticed his undertaking had drawn some bystanders: Weight and his crew, people with nothing better to do, even a few Indians drifting over and perching on the fence rails like curious cats.

Once he'd cinched the saddle, he picked up the bridle and approached his new mount. Softly: "Easy, boy. There ain't gonna be any trouble between us. This is a good rig, bought in St. Louis, Missouri. Along with that saddle it's the only decent thing I ever got out of that godforsaken state." The horse appeared to be listening. He slid the halter over its head. "Try out that bit. You see what I mean? That's quality workmanship. Jes' like you." He knelt and with two quick strokes of his knife severed the lines holding the horse's legs. The onlookers leaned forward in anticipation. "Those people are fools," he murmured, "and we're gonna show 'em up for what they are. We'll waltz out of here just as neat as you please, you and me. We'll show 'em, won't we?" Then, in one swift movement, he was in the saddle, reins gripped in his hand. Not doing anything, just sitting there, letting it get used to his weight.

The bystanders waited, jaws unhinged, expecting the big red bronc to go berserk. But nothing happened.

Not at first.

He tugged the reins and the two of them started away. Animal and rider made one slow circuit of the corral, but the next time around the sorrel noticed another horse, a buckskin mare, on the other side of the fence and reacted with unexpected ferocity. All at once Seaver found himself thrown backward as his steed flung itself at the smaller horse, rearing and striking out with its front hooves.

Seaver could hear the spectators whooping and hollering but he needed no encouragement, hanging on for dear life. In its excitement, the sorrel collided with the intervening rails, nearly tumbling sideways. Seaver yanked on the reins, hearing the bit click sharply between its teeth. "Settle down, *damnit*." His nerves and horsemanship served him well because once the animal righted itself, its behavior was much improved. It understood simple commands. Good. Not stupid, just mean and contrary. He could live with that.

Seaver swapped his old pack horse for a creature that looked part mule. It was plug ugly and sway-backed but it could bear a load and was unlikely to wander off. Perfect for his requirements.

As promised, he rode his new horse off the premises, passing the gawkers on the way out. Suddenly taken aback when he recognized one of their number.

Shorty McGee.

During the course of his travels, Seaver had met many an individual who had been favored with that moniker, but Delbert McGee lived up to it, in spades.

If he was four and a half feet high, someone once joked, it was because Shorty was waving his hands in the air. But such wisecracks were rarely uttered in the little man's presence. He didn't normally encourage such liberties, especially in the company of strangers and greenhorns. Not that he minded a good joke, ol' Shorty, he just didn't like you *harping* on it.

He and Seaver had crossed paths on at least three occasions and as far as he knew, the little man had no quarrel with him. Maybe with the moustache gone—

But Shorty looked and looked again. Smiled, sort of. They exchanged stiff nods and that was it.

Seaver rode on and anyone watching would have noticed nothing immediately amiss except, perhaps, he might have been sitting slightly straighter in the saddle, his shoulders squared, head up.

The change was subtle, barely discernible.

Unless you had an eye for fine detail.

Or possessed the well-honed instincts of a shootist.

"'Lo, Shorty."

Seaver was waiting near a pile of building materials someone had left stacked on the outskirts of the settlement. The future home of some poor, homesick Swede or Mick. Or, maybe not. Folks were saying the place's days were numbered, that with the fort abandoned, the soldiers gone, there was no point staying. Five years, this could be just another ghost town. Tapped out. Wrung dry. The mountains loomed close by; winters here could be hard. The stack of boards looked insubstantial, inadequate to the task.

Shorty was astride a small, dun horse and appeared to be in good spirits, raising a hand in greeting. Seaver recollected that he usually sported a custom-made pistol, fitted for his small mitt. He was relieved the pistol was nowhere in evidence. He'd taken a chance, stuck the Remington in the saddlebag with the Colt. Not that he was *entirely* trusting: there was a twitchy little .41 derringer in his right coat pocket. For emergencies or just in case.

Their horses nosed each other. Seaver's horse—christened, in Ed Weight's honor, the Goddamn Nag—gave a warning snort, which the smaller critter ignored. Like its owner, the diminutive pony was feisty, giving no ground.

"Knew it was you. You was always good with horses. A real natural. You ain't scairt a nothin', that's the most important thing when it comes to critters. It makes them scairt o' *you*." Shorty brought his pony alongside and Seaver leaned over, shook his hand. "It was smart, shaving the moustache off. Marked you like a brand." Grinning up at him. "Heard a few things. Got a minute?"

He nodded and the two of them started north at an easy walk. Shorty was traveling light, not even any saddlebags. Which meant he'd be turning around and heading back to Fetterman. Pity. He was good company and a first rate man to have on your side in a tight spot. Seeing those Indians skulking around the fort reminded him that he was in undiscovered country, as the Bard would say, and there was safety in numbers. "So what's the news?"

"There's this story I hear," Shorty began.

"This ain't the one about the two Irishmen and the farmer's daughter, is it?" Seaver warned and Shorty smirked.

"Naw. This one's better. About a deputy sheriff in St. Joseph, Missouri who got hisself kilt for slappin' leather with...well, let's jes' say someone he shouldn't have. You know that one?"

"Mebbe," Seaver admitted.

"But there's more."

"Thought so."

"The so-called guilty party had already kilt somebody, a known quantity, shall we say, name of Randall Gower. Way I hear it, Gower recognized him and thought he'd make his name by collecting a famous scalp. Only it didn't work out that way. So Gower's dead, our man is walkin' out, as peaceable as you please, and then this deputy, name of Talbot—"

"Talbot," Seaver repeated, committing the name to memory.

"—takes it upon hisself to play hero. Yanks his piece and lets 'er rip. And that's all she wrote."

"He came close. I heard a click, fired right after he did. Never noticed the badge. Just a flash and smoke."

"He didn't say nothin'?"

"*Nothin'*," Seaver insisted, "just pulled and popped one off but it went wild. Nervous. Only a kid. *Damn* him...."

"I suppose you know the boy comes from a good family. Prominent people, I hear. Good friends with the governor." Seaver said nothing. There was nothing to say. "Had all that goin' for him. And now he's dead."

"Now he's dead." They looked at each other.

"*Missouri*. I recollect you sayin' on more than one occasion you'd never set foot in that perticular state again."

"I know."

"I got a real clear memory of you tellin' us about all the bad things that happened to you there."

Seaver shifted in his saddle, seeking a more comfortable position. A different part of his backside to bruise. "It's true. I heard about this high stakes poker game and thought, hell, St. Joe is just across the border. I can always hightail it back to Kansas. I shoulda known better." Glaring down at his companion. "But I swear to God, Shorty, it was an accident. The fool should've...well, it's too late for anything but tears. And I ain't sheddin' any over the likes of him."

"They sent Steubing after you," Shorty said. Casting his eyes at the ground. "Thought you'd like to know."

"Steubing..."

"Payin' him good money to bring you back. On your saddle or over it, they don't profess to care." They had reined in their mounts, still facing north. It was getting on, around four in the afternoon. The temperature dropping; Shorty shivered. "Dang, it's cold. Should be headin' back."

"Anything else?"

Shorty grinned up at him. "Ain't that enough?" And that did it. Their laughter carried for miles, all the way to the mountains and back again.

"It's good to see you again, Shorts." Wiping at his eyes.

"I'll always remember that stampede—"

"All I could see was your hat."

"The way their horns glowed, green like ghost light."

"Somethin' in the air. Spooky. Never seen anything like it."

They spent some companionable moments recalling shared adventures, friends in common. Seaver liked Shorty and considered him one of the bravest men he'd ever met. The night of the stampede, in the midst of the lightning, bawling cattle, shouts and tumult, Shorty was the one who turned the herd. Naked as a jaybird, firing his little pistol, recklessly steering his horse Zeke into the path of certain death, while thunder shouted from overhead, the heavens fit to burst.

Hec Steubing.

Well, there it was.

In the old days it might have been possible to get away with plugging a deputy sheriff or two, especially if they overstepped the line of duty. Nowadays, it was considered a national disgrace and word would race up and down the wire, the posters going out by stagecoach or express, and before long everybody and his aunt back in Dublin knew your face and how much it was worth.

Eventually, men like Steubing, Robert Clayton or Josh Randall would be dispatched, to do their duty and claim their rightful bounty for rendering the world safe for ordinary, decent folks.

From the authorities' point of view, desperados and Indians impeded the course of progress and, therefore, neither could be tolerated. Their existence an affront to civilization. Railroads wouldn't lay track where there was no rule of law: savages on the warpath, villains and desperate men halting trains and robbing passengers and baggage, behaving in defiance of reason and decency. Nothing that interfered with the exchange of goods and services or disrupted the ebb and flow of capital would be countenanced.

The West was changing. Hell, the whole country was changing. The bankers and lawyers ran things now; even the old cattle barons had been subjugated, absorbed by the rising business class. He played poker with a fellow from Pittsburgh who claimed it would be oil men rising to the top of the heap next. Wells and derricks were springing up everywhere back east, despoiling the landscape, poisoning water, people falling all over themselves trying to get rich quick, treating the filthy goo with the same kind of excitement and greed that gold commanded. It was only a matter of time before oil fever spread west of the Missouri.

Seaver devoutly hoped that never came to pass and suspected Hec Steubing would sympathize with that sentiment. He, too, belonged to another era, a good old boy likely well acquainted with the hill country where Seaver's people still made their home. His duties took him far afield and he wasn't harried by boundaries and jurisdictions. A no-nonsense sort of fellow, if his reputation was accurate.

Methodical, dogged, a man with ice water for blood. The prototype of a first rate bounty hunter.

"Leastways you know he won't by lyin' in the weeds somewhere," Shorty had offered, by way of consolation. "He ain't no bushwhacker."

Steubing was renowned for his scrupulous fairness. He'd try to take you alive if he could and if you chose to offer resistance, contest his authority, it would be a standup fight. He favored his right hand, rode big horses and was equally adept with rifle and pistol. The number of men he had killed or maimed ranged from fifteen to forty, depending on who was doing the telling and their state of inebriation. One story, possibly apocryphal, had him turning down a job with the Texas Rangers, rebuffing them by stating that he preferred to work independently, adding "sometimes a badge can cramp a man's style".

Seaver, in a pinch, had pinned on a tin star twice but it didn't take. Wearing a badge was lousy, demeaning work and no one—not the mayor, the local merchants, most especially the citizens you were supposed to be protecting— gave you a nickel's worth of credit for doing your job. Every day you put your life on the line and for what? Ninety dollars a month and free room and board, sometimes in a conveniently empty cell that still stank of the drunken cowboy who'd slept there the night before.

After each brief sabbatical on the right side of the law he was always eager to return to his former bad habits. With that desire came a renewed sense that he didn't much *like* the average person, and then the added realization that he'd rather be a so-called "bad man" than offer his services to the likes of them.

The following afternoon his packhorse (which, owing to

its lack of personality, he had yet to name) began favoring its right front leg. One look told him all he needed to know. The shoe was bent, hanging from a single nail. He fetched some pliers and pried it loose. From what he could see, the shoe was salvageable so he kept it, rather than flinging it into the brush in frustration, which was his first inclination. He was preoccupied and the Nag took the opportunity, once it felt his foot in the stirrup, to twist around and nip at him, receiving a profane-laced rebuke for its presumption.

Good fortune was with him because a short time later he spied a thin, curling line of smoke and soon emerged into a clearing containing a small, sturdy farmhouse backing on to a splashing creek. The water would be cold and pure, originating from further up in the mountains, hanging glaciers of ancient snow and ice.

The farmer's name was Klaus Brunig or Bruning, it was hard to make it out through his thick German accent. He spoke some English, not much, his wife, Hilda, even less. The daughter, Inger, was a plain, dumpy thing, of marrying age and likely a good catch if you weren't choosy or gifted with halfway decent eyesight. The best *she* could manage was "Yes?" and "Hello". There had been a son, apparently, but he was gone. Either dead or run off. He was mentioned only once and their faces darkened, the memory of whatever happened to him still fresh in their minds.

Like most men who, due to their isolated circumstances, had to rely on their own devices, Bruning or Brunig was a jack of all trades, including smithing. The shoe was pounded, straightened and back on by suppertime. By then the light was failing and his hosts, plainly starved for company, made it clear that he was expected to stay overnight. Not wanting to show ingratitude for their hospitality, he agreed to share their table and linger there until morning. Due to the cramped state of their abode it meant he would have to bed down in the barn, a crude affair that sheltered what little stock they had and preserved their stores of grain and seed from the elements. He could see through the roof in places and the hay smelt of damp and thicker, deeper odors.

To make up for the primitive accommodations, Hilda set a fine table: there was smoked venison, root vegetables and some kind of porridge or gruel made with ground oats and honey. Preserves for dessert.

"A repast fit for royalty," Seaver complimented her at one point, receiving a look of utter incomprehension in response.

"My vife does not English," her husband reminded their visitor and Seaver nodded, feeling like a halfwit. It could have been that he was distracted. Inger had been making cow eyes at him all through supper, playing footsie with him under the table. Then, using the tablecloth for cover, she reached over and placed her hand on his leg, leaving it there for several long, tantalizing seconds. Her parents seemed oblivious to what was going on. The girl, somewhere between sixteen and her early twenties, didn't inspire erotic thoughts, not even when she brushed against him as she was clearing the table, offering him a good look at her ample bosom. It was at that point that Klaus cottoned on to what she was up to and barked at her, a cutting, guttural remark that sent her scurrying away in tears.

Unfortunately, that wasn't the end of it.

After he'd bade the family good night and claimed his spot next to a stall occupied by an old brood mare, he laid down in his musty bed and awaited the inevitable.

An hour later, the farmyard and its environs draped in darkness, he heard the front door creak open. He fervently hoped it was merely one of the family making a nocturnal visit to the privy...but the outhouse was east of the house and that wasn't where the footfalls were heading.

He sat up but was surprised to discover it was *Hilda* Brunig (or Bruning) peering in the doorway, seeking him out. Her nightdress was white, giving the visitation a spectral aspect. At last her eyes adjusted and she moved to take a step inside.

"Yes?"

"No." His tone was firm, brooking no argument. Trailing disappointment and frustration, she made her way to the privy. He was glad she hadn't pressed her case. A domestic dispute could turn ugly very quickly and he had no wish to test the farmer's mettle. His life was fraught with complication as it was and a few minutes of pleasure hardly seemed worth the trouble that might result from what amounted, literally, to a roll in the hay.

You really are getting old, he told himself.

Or more picky.

Drifting off while still trying to make up his mind which of the two alternatives was closest to the truth.

CHAPTER TWO

IT WAS HARD TO determine where and when he entered the Montana Territory. There were no signs posted and the local chamber of commerce neglected to send anyone out to officially greet him. He tried not to hold it against them.

Immense stands of trees lined the route north; some were true giants, hundreds of feet tall and seemingly indifferent to the passing of the ages. It was a region of fast-running rivers and long ranges of impressive hills descending into lush, green valleys, the land rising the further west you ventured. A wide variety of wildlife, ample forage, spectacular scenery: perhaps it really *was* Eden.

But unlike Adam, he wasn't alone. Seaver passed scattered farmhouses and homesteads but no towns of any note. Few facilities for travelers, such amenities in this part of the country largely an afterthought. He didn't miss them.

It's still a frontier, Seaver marveled. Nobody had filled in the countryside with church spires and rowhouses or laid out ruler straight streets with raised wooden sidewalks. When you took a breath, you were breathing real air, uncontaminated by the sour stench of civilization.

Most of all, there were no fences, delineating property lines. Fences meant neighbors, people living in close proximity, suspicious of strangers and jealously protective of the things that were *theirs*. The man who invented barbed wire should've been strung up by his boot heels. He recollected hearing the Indians referred to it as "devil's rope". Rightly so.

A four-strand fence separated you from the rest of the world, like a border that had to be secured and protected against invasion. Sacred ground. Defended to the *death*, if necessary.

The Civil War had taught him the fallacy of that kind of thinking. Mine and yours. Us and them. He was too young to have served but one-legged Uncle Rafe was an unimpeachable authority on the terrible consequences of armed conflict. The toll in human life. If there was any glory in pitting mass armies against each other, giving them free rein to slaughter the opposition with the latest weapons and strategies, it sure didn't show itself at Antietam or Bull Run.

The conflict colored his childhood, the four-year campaign incurring terrible losses on his extended family and community. As a youth, he attended too many funerals and came to hold the same view as most in his home county: war was an enterprise led by damn fools who killed by proxy and eluded blame afterward.

Mass slaughter didn't ennoble men, it *brutalized* them. God knows, he'd seen ample evidence of that.

The first man he'd ever killed boasted that he'd been Jeb Stuart's best lieutenant and "the bravest soul to don the Gray 'cept ol' Robert E. Lee hisself". Yet the experience clearly hadn't done him any credit. There he was, propped up on the end of the bar, a mean, worthless drunk. His rheumy eyes fixed on a seventeen-year-old kid who was the only one in the dingy saloon bold enough to return his gaze.

"You lookin' at me, boy?" Before anyone could intervene, he was hauling out a huge pistol, a regular hogleg, intending to send the kid and anyone else in the vicinity on a one-way trip to the hereafter. At the time, Seaver was unarmed except for a Barlow pocketknife. The ex-soldier's first shot exploded bottles behind the bar and everyone but Seaver dove for cover, a melee of shouts and overturned tables. The pistol was old, its action stiff. In the time it took his assailant to crank back the hammer, steady his pistol and take better aim, Seaver knelt down, snatched a .44 from the man nearest him and shot the drunk in the chest, killing him instantly.

He recalled the incident with perfect clarity. The stunned looks on the faces of the men who raised their heads from the floor or wherever they'd sought refuge. The screams of the barmaid. The plume of smoke that hovered in the air, drifting up toward the ceiling, carrying with it the unmistakable aroma of gunplay.

How had he felt? What word best described his state of mind as he joined the others, examining the body on the rough, wood floor, a bullet hole directly over the heart, puddle of bright blood spreading beneath it, trickling across the filthy boards?

Serenity.

Once he'd ascertained that the drunk's associates had no inclination to seek vengeance, he returned the pistol to its owner and beat a hasty retreat. While the fault clearly rested with the dead man, he had no wish, even at that tender age, to risk his freedom, possibly his *life*, on the vicissitudes of western jurisprudence.

Hannibal, Missouri. Nearly two decades ago now.

Seaver never learned the man's name or if he really had served as he'd claimed. He was the first but not the last. As his proficiency with weapons improved, his reputation grew along with it. Soon discovering that there was a fellowship of professional gunmen and a pecking order that went with it (albeit one constantly being amended due to the high casualty rate of those in that chosen profession).

Hickok and the James boys, Ben Thompson and John

Wesley Hardin, all were famous in their time, their exploits, often exaggerated, enshrined in myth and legend. The type of men commemorated in Beadle dime novels and immortalized in the pale, pink pages of the *Police Gazette*: larger than life and too good to be true.

But there was a separate roster, made up of individuals whose names weren't printed but *whispered*, men who did not require the trappings of fame and notoriety, all the trouble that attracted. Stone cold killers, most of them, guns for hire if the price was right and they were so disposed. A good number, like Seaver, had seen the law from both sides and couldn't discern any difference between those who chose a life of crime and those who meted out punishment. West of the Missouri a man was his own lawyer, judge and, if need be, executioner as well.

Such individuals didn't keep a running tally of the opponents they'd faced down and sent to their Maker. It was said that Billy Bonney had twenty-one notches carved into the handle of his pistol but there were some Seaver knew who'd killed *twice* that number, often not discriminating between armed combatants and innocent bystanders. Men and women, even the occasional child falling victim to their indiscriminate zest for killing.

Murderous personalities like "Pie" Jonson, who collected scalps like the fiercest Apache and, when he was well into his cups, bragged that he'd killed more white men than Quantrill and Bloody Bill combined, not to mention at least a hundred Indians. "But, of course," he'd hastily admit, "them Injuns don't really count."

How would Cody or Bat Masterson stand up against that kind of callous nonchalance and contempt for human life?

Seaver's views toward "our red brethren" (as he'd once

heard a Presbyterian minister refer to them) were complicated. On the one hand, he admired their independent nature and courageous resistance against the encroachments of greedy outsiders. Like him, they had little use for the fancy trappings folks found so indispensible nowadays. A practical people, they ate when they were hungry, used only what they required and abhorred senseless waste. They did not seem to aspire to conspicuous wealth or wish to conform to the white man's ways. Good for them.

On the other hand, he had no desire to part with what remained of his hair.

Truthfully, he had only ever socialized with one Indian, Henry Skenontou, an Iroquois he fell in with during his days as a cattleman. Never mind that they weren't his cattle and, strictly speaking, he didn't own so much as a cubit of pasture for them to forage on. Missouri again. All the crazy stuff usually centered around Missouri. *Or when I was drinking*, he reminded himself. Usually both.

Skenontou—he even spelled his name for Seaver's benefit—could read and write and was a fair hand at arithmetic. The product of Jesuit schooling back East. Small, wiry and fairly light-skinned. Henry did his best to disguise his roots and blend in, keeping his long braid tucked down the back of his shirt, hat pulled low over his dark eyes.

He could usually fool most people, pass for a mixed blood Mex, but the night Seaver met him (in some dive near the Kansas-Missouri border), his luck ran out. A shaggy, shifty-eyed hombre who reeked worse than a muleskinner took one look at Henry's profile and didn't like what he saw. Seaver recognized what was about to happen from his position on the Indian's right. He was nursing his second beer and a pernicious hangover from the previous night's festivities. Not in the best of moods, wanting the minimum of noise and grief.

"I smell an *Injun*," the troublemaker piped up. "You don't serve *Injuns* in here, do you, Tony?"

The bartender quit what he was doing and came over to stand directly in front of Henry. An ugly, vicious man, known to stash a lethal knobkerry under the bar to tame troublesome cowboys. "That so? You—*out!*"

Later, Seaver wondered why he involved himself. The hangover was definitely a contributing factor but he had previously shown little interest in the racial makeup of the drinking establishments he favored. "Why doesn't everybody here mind his own damn business and let the man drink?"

Henry flicked a glance at Seaver, sizing up his new ally.

The jasper at the end of the bar wasn't dissuaded, banging a meaty fist down hard enough to quiet the room. "To hell with you, mister! I ain't sharing the same air as this savage, this—" He reeled off a string of epithets that would've bruised the ears of more sensitive types.

"Step out of the way," Seaver told Henry, who was only too happy to comply. He drew back his coat, revealing his Colt and indicating his readiness to use it. At that moment someone got the drunk's ear and urgently explained the situation. He excused himself and made for the exit, moving at a good clip despite his advanced state of intoxication.

Henry and Seaver nodded to each other and returned to their positions at the bar. The evening passed without further incident.

He and Henry partnered together, on and off, for nearly a year. Ol' Henry wasn't much of a horseman but he was strong as two oxen and seemed to have been born without fear. His stout heart and quick wits saved them from the noose on at least three occasions. He was an uncomplaining traveling companion and dependable workmate. Together, they made a good team—both, by nature, taciturn men, exchanging little personal information, content with long, companionable silences, nods and discreet gestures transmitting entire paragraphs with admirable economy.

It wasn't friendship but something like it. Neither man ever used the word; they were *partners*, that's what they called themselves right up to the day Henry left. After almost a decade, he had finally saved enough for a first class train ticket home.

"Goin' back to New Yawk state," he said, still hardly believing it. The two of them sharing an awkward moment before Henry boarded at the station in Kansas City.

"Do they treat Indians any better there?"

Henry stared at Seaver as if he was daft, then stepped up on to the waiting car. They raised a hand to each other and that was it. Earlier, the conductor had been eying Henry, a look that spoke volumes. There was going to be trouble somewhere down the line but Henry had a valid ticket, which entitled him to a sleeping compartment to himself, not to mention all the amenities he would require on the trip to Albany and, eventually, a reservation up near the Canadian border. Where, Henry claimed, it snowed eight months of the year and the trees leaked maple syrup...

He suspected the hazy line of mountains to the west were likely the Bighorns and kept his eyes peeled for anything that seemed amiss. But Seaver saw few signs of Indians—which didn't necessarily mean there weren't any about. They'd had centuries of experience dealing with white people and were smart enough to make themselves scarce if there were any in the vicinity. He wondered what would happen if he ventured from the main trail, strayed into the dark woods of pine and spruce. Would he be swallowed up by the forest, like a lost child in a fairy tale? Borne off by magical forces, leaving no traces?

Not long ago, this region had been the domain of the Sioux, who had driven out their mortal enemies, the Crow and Blackfeet, claiming sole dominion of the land from here to the sacred Black Hills.

Routing the Seventh Cavalry created a terrible backlash, the lunatic Custer elevated to martyr status, blame for the deaths of over two hundred troopers laid at the feet of desperate people intent on defending their territory and way of life. Punitive expeditions were mounted against the Sioux, while eastern newspapers pounded war drums, baying for blood. Avenging armies swept through the great northern plains, dispatched to remind the Indians who called the shots. A number of prominent leaders—Crazy Horse among them—were rounded up and either killed or imprisoned.

The U.S. Army, urged on by its allies and powerful patrons, was hell-bent on exacting revenge for its fallen comrades. Villages of suspected belligerents were attacked, the guilty and the innocent, armed and unarmed, killed without discrimination, murdered with the tacit approval of the powers that be.

But Sitting Bull and many of those present the day Custer fell melted away, slipping across the border into Canada, requesting sanctuary from the Great Mother, Queen Victoria. The British and Canadian governments dithered and delayed and the warmongers gnashed their teeth, biding their time while Custer's assassin hid beneath Vicky's starched skirts.

Washington might be satisfied that the Indian nations

were pacified, its absolute authority reconfirmed, but Seaver was willing to bet there were still plenty of warriors wandering these hills who might beg to differ. The Great Chief in the White House claimed legal title as far as the Western sea, but it sure would be interesting to see him come out here and actually try to *enforce* it.

"A piece of paper don't mean much to an Indian," Henry told him once. "Just something to wipe himself with after he's done his business." He wondered aloud about the white man's fascination with gold. The Black Hills were, apparently, full of it, which was what brought Custer sniffing around in the first place. "It's just dust," Henry marveled, "try to hold it in your hand, squeeze it..." He blew on his fingers to illustrate his point. "You can't eat it if you're hungry or wear it when you're cold."

Seaver tried to explain but even to his own ears it sounded idiotic. This insane desire to possess as much, yes, *dust* as one could amass and to perdition with honesty and charity. Men and a good many women would kill to possess a few *ounces* of the stuff. Enough to convert into nuggets or dangle around your neck. A bauble that dripped blood.

It was clear from his encounter with Shorty that Montana wouldn't be nearly far enough away to suit his purposes. Not if Hec Steubing was after him. Which left following Sitting Bull's example and heading into the Great Northwest. Crossing the border and never returning to his native soil.

It was the one place Titus had yet to visit and he told Seaver he regretted the oversight. "It's all Indians and half-breeds up there," he offered by way of endorsement. "Good cattle country. Wide open, like Kansas. Winters are hard, but a man can get used to anything. Leastways that's my experience."

"Do they still have buffalo?" Seaver asked him.

Titus was well into his cups by that point, having nearly polished off the tarantula juice. "You a hunter?"

"I just want to see those critters the way they used to be. The herds that went on forever."

The old prospector went silent. Stared morosely into the fire for a spell, then: "Mister, you ever find a place like that, send word to me. That's a sight I surely would like to witness 'fore I draw my last breath and join my Maker." The flames refusing to relinquish his gaze. His next words scarcely a whisper: "Yessir, that sure would be somethin'."

CHAPTER THREE

THEN THERE WAS the day Frank Seaver encountered Dwayne Farnsworth.

It was well into August and he was somewhere south of Billings, where he planned to stop for provisions and rest the animals. They were bearing up well and though the Nag still displayed the occasional bout of ill humor, nipping and butting with its head, Seaver was satisfied the gelding had turned out to be a first-rate investment. Strong and limber, built for distance.

It was right around the time he usually thought about making camp, the light turning golden and diffuse. He'd made good progress despite a lengthy detour to avoid a sizeable forest fire. The scenery was very much to his liking, verdant hills rolling downward into a broad basin, colorful with late blooming wildflowers. It was like the countryside was showing off its wares, the hillsides painted in every imaginable hue: spikes of blue and pink larkspur, clusters of alpine azalea; drooping, purple bells of mountain heather.

It made for dazzling viewing.

The path took him into the trees, pine mostly, surrounding him with a rich, living scent. Within a few hundred yards the cover began to thin and he entered a clearing, a peaceful bower that had provided rest and respite to many a weary traveler. There was evidence of prior human habitation, felled trees and stacked wood. The ground was level and provided ample space for horses.

It was an ideal location for stopping.

Unfortunately, it was already occupied.

But as soon as the camp's lone resident spotted Seaver, the reaction was swift and enthusiastic.

"Hidee! Hidee! I got grub, I got coffee!" The figure practically kicking his heels together and capering when he saw that Seaver was steering his horses toward the encampment. "You sure is welcome, I'll tell you that. Come on down and let's break bread. What d'you say to that?"

Seaver pulled up about fifteen feet away, pretending to work a crick out of his neck. Meanwhile, surveying the area. It was a neat camp, good location, a trickle of water announcing a spring or creek in the vicinity.

"Howdy," he offered by way of greeting. Remaining seated for the time being.

"Name's Dee-wayne Farnsworth and don't mind if it is." He appeared to be little more than a boy. Seventeen years old or thereabouts and used to living rough by the look of it. Filthy, snaggle-haired, bare of foot, his tattered pants held up by a frayed length of twine. A rack of bony ribs only partially concealed by a shirt missing all but two buttons and at least three sizes too big.

Seaver liked that the kid stayed where he was, not bounding forward with his hand outstretched or making any sudden movements. It was best they had an opportunity to get acquainted. He could see the lad was having a hard time keeping still, shifting from one foot to the other, clearly delighted that the forest trail had produced an unexpected visitor. Those feet had covered a lot of ground, by the look of it. There were boots over by the fire pit but they looked too small for him. Farnsworth followed his eyes and his face brightened. "You want some grub? Hungry? Man, I got enough to feed purt near the entire Seventh Cavalry. C'mon down, what you waitin' for?"

Seaver's gaze left the boots and moved on to the rest of

the boy's gear. Something was wrong. The whole scene left him uneasy. Farnsworth edged toward the fire, always facing his visitor. "I don't mind sharin'. We're both white men, ain't we?"

"I got some tasty jerky," Seaver finally offered.

"Well, there you go! Meat is one thing I ain't got. I looked, but..." He paused, watching the rider dismount. As Seaver swung down, he poked the Nag with the toe of his boot, causing the animal to swing about in irritation, its broad body positioned between the two men.

"Dang horse," he complained, "set still why don't you?" He reached into the saddlebag, rummaged around. "This horse ain't been nothin' but trouble since I bought him."

"Shore seems an uppity brute."

"Ornery as hell. Might be the breed, except I ain't exactly sure what breed it is." Earlier it had had been overcast, threatening rain. He was wearing the .44 Remington under his range coat, a knee-length duster with flap pockets. He kept his right hand tucked in one of those pockets as he approached, lobbing the kid the jerky with his left. Farnsworth caught the bag, sniffed it speculatively.

"That's fine, mister. Real fine. And I thank ye for sharing it with your humble servant." He was closely scrutinizing the older man, sizing him up. Some part of the kid's anatomy was constantly in motion, his body twitching with suppressed energy or excitement. He crouched down, grasped the skillet, grunting in annoyance when the wooden handle came off in his hand, spilling three or four biscuits into the dirt. He had to check and see if there was coffee in the pot, sloshing it speculatively.

"Fine place to camp," Seaver observed. He knelt and with his free hand retrieved one of the fallen biscuits. It was hard and cold. Might as well try chewing one of the nearby trees. Farnsworth, meanwhile, was tearing off strips of jerky and cramming it into his mouth. Small, stained teeth gnawed the stiff, stringy meat. The fire had burned down and would have to be built up before dark. He wondered why the boy hadn't seen to it yet. The cold settled in fast up here. "*Dee-wayne*..." The kid stiffened. "Not sure I know anybody who goes by that name."

The boy settled back, resting on his haunches. "That's 'cause it's really just 'Dwayne'. But my step-mama used to call me that. '*Dee*-wayne! Where ya at, boy?' '*Dee*-wayne, your daddy gonna give you a good hidin'." Mimicking a shrill, female scold.

"So why d'you hang on to it?"

"As a reminder. So's I don't ever forget the old biddy. She called me that right up to the day I left."

"She treat you bad?"

"Only like a *dog*. There weren't no other young 'uns around and no niggers neither so that made me the hired help. I don't remember nothin' but work and bein' hungry all the time."

"A regular David Copperfield."

"Who's that?" The kid regarding him sharpish. "You sportin' with me, mister?"

"Not hardly."

"You gonna eat that biscuit?"

"Here." Seaver tossed it to him. Farnsworth tried breaking off a piece but didn't make much of a dent. Finally flinging it away in contempt.

"Leave it for the danged bears." He giggled. "If they're so inclined, which I doubt." He pointed at Seaver's pocket, the hand it conspicuously contained. "You got somethin' else in there? Somethin' yer savin'?"

"Tobacco fixings."

Dwayne Farnsworth nearly swooned. "Mister, every word you speak is golden. You got some 'baccy in there? You got papers too? I'll roll us both a quirly, you want. My daddy taught me how."

Seaver thought about it, then slipped his hand out of his pocket, the tobacco pouch visible in his fingers.

It was what the kid had been waiting for. With one preternaturally quick movement, his hand darted over his left shoulder and was sweeping forward when a dot the size of a penny appeared on his upper lip and his head was violently thrown back by the impact of a .41 caliber bullet. He shuddered violently and toppled forward onto the hard-packed dirt at Seaver's feet.

A short dagger lay a foot or so in front of his body. It appeared handmade, its handle carved from some kind of bone, the blade thin and pointed. A regular Arkansas toothpick, plucked from a shoulder or neck sheath he'd secreted beneath his baggy shirt. When he picked it up, Seaver found it was perfectly balanced, the product of many hours of diligent labor. He tested the edge, nicking his palm in the process. *Sharp.*

The nickel-plated derringer had saved his bacon. He'd taken the opportunity to slide it up his sleeve when he'd retrieved the tobacco from his kit, the Nag's body covering the exchange. So that once the kid made his move, all he had to do was let go of the pouch and the piece dropped into his hand, ready for action.

He'd suspected Farnsworth from the start. That said, the kid's speed surprised him. If he'd been a beat or two slower, it would be the boy standing over *him*, watching his life's blood seeping into the ground, feeding the root systems of the surrounding trees. Once again, his naturally suspicious nature and hair-trigger reflexes had saved the day.

The kid tried to play it smart, no question, but too much gave him away. His eyes most of all. The sharp, watchful eyes of a predator, calculating and cruel. He didn't belong to the camp, that much was obvious from the start. He was an interloper, which begged the question: *what happened to the original occupant?*

So right away he knew he was facing a killer. There were many varieties of that species, something else two decades in the business had taught him. He figured the kid had a knife, made sure he never got too close, effectively forcing him to throw it. That bought some time and a damn good thing too.

"You should've tried squeezing into them boots," Seaver told the prone figure, the boy's eyes dull, lusterless, his skin rapidly losing color. "Messed up the camp some too. It's too neat and tidy for the likes of you."

The boots. The camp. The busted pot handle and cold biscuits. It all clearly pointed to another party.

It didn't take long to find the owner. He had been dragged into the bush about twenty yards away. His throat was deftly cut so obviously a trusting soul to let the kid get that close. It hadn't happened long before he'd come along. The victim's face wore a disappointed expression, his limbs stiffening, as if resisting further insult.

His name was Victor Karlson and in his wallet was a daguerrotype of his wife. She looked homely but kind. There were papers, bills of lading. Sealed and notarized documents, several bound in blue ribbons. Mr. Karlson had been on some kind of business trip, his journey rudely interrupted. No sign of a horse, the attack must have spooked it and caused it to run off. Bad luck for the kid. There were two letters, presumably to Karlson's wife. A Colorado address. He'd see they got mailed at the first opportunity, along with whatever he could take with him. Not much else he could do. The case had been moved to a court of higher authority.

It was getting dark. He needed to get the bodies under ground as quick as he could. He wished he could leave the kid to the elements. But these woods were home to large carnivores, sure to be drawn to the smell of fresh blood. He got a short spade from the pack horse, commenced work. The ground was hard and heavily rooted.

Karlson's funeral was, by necessity, perfunctory and unaccompanied by words or rites. He didn't feel qualified. Just a shallow hole and the dignity of being out of the reach of scavengers. Farnsworth he merely rolled into a trench, tossing a few loose spadefuls of dirt on him, resisting the urge to spit on his handiwork afterwards.

As soon as he was done, he got the fire going, huddling up close. Endured a bad bout of the shakes. It had been a close call. Closer than he dared admit. Another sign he was getting old. He tried some of the jerky but didn't have a taste for it. He let the fire die down, climbed into his roll and tried to sleep.

But it was a long time coming.

His bones woke first and kept complaining until the rest of him took notice. He'd been violently thrown from horses, suffered various accidents and drunken mishaps and it had done something to his back. Knocked it out of alignment. He always paid the price when sleeping rough.

Throwing aside his covering wraps, *creaking* as he sat up, his lower spine objecting strenuously. Sucking in the cool, morning air to keep from groaning. He detected movement at the edge of the clearing. His rifle was within reach, a round already chambered. Turning his head slowly but ready to react instantly at the first sign of a threat—

The stag was enormous, almost a third larger than the Nag. *My God*, Seaver thought, *is* everything *bigger in Montana*?

The creature seemed unconcerned by his presence. It tugged at some leaves just above its head, maneuvering carefully because of its heavy, jutting antlers. A trophy set.

Yet Seaver never gave a moment's thought to reaching for the rifle. Forty yards away, even an amateur could have potted it. But one shot likely wouldn't bring down something of that size, he'd need a larger caliber weapon, like a Sharps. And if he shot wrong, he'd have to track it through the woods, following the trail of blood deeper and deeper into the wild, perhaps getting lost and dying along with his prey.

And it would serve me right, he decided. It was so magnificent. Killing it would be a crime against nature, a sin that could never be expiated. He stayed where he was, just watching it. He could smell the huge buck from that position, a sour, earthy musk he would always remember.

Finally the stag had eaten its fill and prepared to return to the forest. Somehow it detected him, pausing to regard him with a long, inscrutable gaze. Then it swung around and disappeared into the trees.

"Thank you," Frank Seaver whispered, though it was unclear exactly who or what he was addressing. The stag? The morning? God?

Could any religion or creed encompass the reverence the creature inspired merely by *existing*, or duplicate the stillness at the center of his soul he'd experienced from the moment it wandered into the clearing? He felt honored, *blessed* by its presence and the morning took on new significance, touched by glory, imbued with magic and possibility.

Now that he had the luxury of daylight, Seaver took more care with Victor Karlson's gravesite. He fetched rocks, as many as he could find, piling them on the low mound until he figured he'd done all he could to protect it from all but the most determined marauder. Dwayne Farnsworth's final resting place didn't warrant similar consideration. He was partially uncovered, his bare feet sticking out. It wouldn't be long before something got at him.

"Damn your soul forever," Seaver growled. "You weren't fit for life and it was a pleasure killin' you." It was the most satisfactory eulogy he could manage on such short notice.

He went through Karlson's gear, setting aside everything worth salvaging, stowing it in a duffel he found. The authorities would see to it that his missus was informed of his ignoble fate. His people should know that he wouldn't be coming home and the circumstances of his death. It would come as little comfort to them but at least it would be something.

The waiting was the worst. For some, the bad news would merely confirm a secret knowledge their heart somehow acquired long before word finally arrived.

Their grieving had already begun.

The path here was well traveled, a narrow swale worn by horses and wagons, the ruts plainly visible. A significant amount of traffic came through this way, bound for Billings and then, most likely, Oregon and California.

It was around noon when he came upon the boy. He was perched on a low bough of a tree, swinging his feet listlessly, paying no mind as Seaver reined in beside him.

"Hey, there, sonny, you live around here?" The child

raised his face and Seaver saw his eyes were puffy with expended grief.

"Lemme alone. Go 'way."

"You got folks?" The lad didn't answer. "You all right?"

"Jes' leave me be, mister." Turning his face away. Inconsolable, not interested in his sympathy.

Seaver smelled the homestead before he saw it. A mixture of outdoor privy, wood smoke and animals kept in close quarters. The house, built with peeled logs, was roughhewn but solid. The yard was well maintained, its owners expending considerable time and energy clearing the area, removing even the stumps of the vast trees that once stood here. The house and property spoke of admirable industry and tireless work, the kind of supreme effort that surviving in such hardscrabble circumstances required.

But when he rode up, the place was silent, an ominous lull. There should have been barnyard noises, the lowing and squawking of creatures kept for sustenance. And some mongrel dog, snapping at the Nag's heels, a sentinel and companion. The quiet made him uneasy and he kept one hand on the butt of the Remington as he slow-walked his horse toward the dwelling.

There was smoke coming from the chimney and an impression of watching eyes. Which came as something of a relief. He'd been worried he'd stumbled across a charnel house, the boy the sole survivor of a massacre. He called out a greeting and the front door, hung with leather hinges and as sturdy as the rest of the structure, edged partway open.

"Whachu want?"

"Everything all right here? Just passing through and I thought—"

A scrawny man emerged, his attitude cautious. He snugged his suspenders over bony, sunburnt shoulders, eying Seaver suspiciously. "What's that, mister? I got a mind to fetch my Parker 'less you make your business clear."

"Name's Thornton. Like I said, just passing through."

"Best be on your way then. No need for tarryin'."

"I just saw your boy."

"Caleb? Where he at?"

"In a tree, yonder. Lookin' like he's lost his best friend." Pausing. "You don't look much better, truth be told."

The farmer gestured vaguely. "Well...we had ourselfs a bad night."

"He kilt Joey." A girl, no more than five years old, stood in the crooked doorway. "That's why Caleb's sad." Joining her father on the porch.

"That's right, honey," he agreed, patting her head.

"And the chickens."

The farmer swallowed. "He did that too."

Seaver leaned forward. "Did he go by the name of *Dee-wayne* Farnsworth?"

That got their attention. "That's the bas—that's who done it. You know him?"

"I met him," Seaver said.

"He was a bad boy," the little girl stated.

Seaver nodded, looking at her daddy, speaking directly to him. "Not any more he ain't." He sensed another presence, looked down as the boy materialized beside him. "And you're Caleb, is that right?"

The Kaline family seemed determined to spoil him. Tom kept thanking him and offering him more of his home made hooch and Caleb fell all over himself, so anxious to please. Little Sally even got into the spirit, hauling herself up into his lap and refusing to be budged. Brazenly plucking out his pocket watch, amusing herself by flipping it open and closed, asking about the writing inside and if it was from his wife. When Tom chided her, Seaver answered truthfully that the timepiece held no sentimental value and only worked half the time anyway. He showed her how to wind it, holding it to her ear so she could hear it ticking.

It took repeated visits behind a cotton sheet drawn across one corner of the interior. Finally, Margaret Kaline was persuaded to rally herself and join them. She seemed the worst off of the bunch. A slight, small-boned woman, the events of the previous twenty-four hours had clearly taken their toll on her. After the family's encounter with Farnsworth, she had retreated into prayer, relying on her faith to sustain her.

"I've heard about evil, Mr. Thornton," she told him, "but until I met that boy I never encountered it face to face."

He'd come down the trail, claiming to hail from Bozeman originally but, truly, he was a demon escaped from the deepest precinct of hell. Caleb saw him first and came in to inform her there was a stranger outside, begging for food or work or both. Margaret retrieved her husband's Parker shotgun before going out to meet their visitor.

They'd seen all kinds roaming up and down the trail, good folk and desperate ones and everything in between. Margaret had become a quick and astute judge of character and it only took one look at Farnsworth to put her on guard.

From the threshold she told him that her husband was out back but since the light was failing he was welcome to some food and, if he wasn't particular, could bed down in the chicken coop. The boy didn't seem enamored with the suggestion and whined about how hungry and cold he was and how downright grateful he'd be for a good, home-cooked meal, shared with a fine, God-fearing family such as theirs. She said she'd be happy to send him out some victuals, but that her husband adamantly refused to allow strangers under their roof.

"That ain't too neighborly," he complained, his demeanor quickly turning surly. She sensed him eying her up, made sure he saw the twelve-gauge, which definitely made an impression. Just then Tom, who really *had* been out back, chose an opportune moment to come around the front of the house, his claw hammer hooked in his belt, and she could see Farnsworth reconsidering his options. Coming to the conclusion the coop was acceptable after all, sending back effusive thanks when Caleb took him out his supper plate.

Tom thought Margaret was being unduly callous with regards to the lad and said so but she remained resolute. Before turning in, she barred the door and securely latched the shutters. Her husband asked if she was expecting to be besieged by bloodthirsty redskins but she didn't rise to the bait. Tom was soon sound asleep, not a care in the world. Margaret remained awake and alert and in the wee hours her vigilance was rewarded. She heard a board creak outside and then detected a light tread working its way along the exterior of the house. She gripped Tom's arm but other than a murmur of complaint, he paid her no mind.

The prowler reconnoitered the house, inspecting the two small windows for points of entry. But Tom had done his job well and the shutters resisted his persistent probing. The front door was solid and though their visitor circled the dwelling twice, he found no easy way inside. She sensed his growing frustration. Finally, she heard him withdraw, muttering to himself.

They didn't discover the depth of his fury until the following morning when Caleb went outside to do his business. He called his dog, Joey, but the animal wouldn't come, so Caleb went looking for him.

They heard him cry out and went to discover the cause. Joey's body had been cruelly treated—they didn't describe the injuries out of consideration for the boy—but Dwayne Farnsworth hadn't stopped there.

The Kaline family had recently taken delivery of twenty-five juvenile chickens, shipped in willow cages from Billings. The long journey took its toll (they had originally ordered *fifty*). Farnsworth descended on them in their small, boxed-in enclosure, lined with whatever fabric the family had on hand to insulate it from the cold. He'd slain them all, sparing none. The pullets had been a significant investment of time and money and their demise meant a loss of eggs and meat that would have serious ramifications come winter. All that was left was a mass of bloody feathers and an unmistakable residue of maniacal rage.

"I never seen such a thing," Tom Kaline whispered. "He cut their heads off, every last one. Left 'em in a little pile for us to find. And then poor Joey..."

"I'm glad you kilt him," Caleb said, his expression fierce. "I wish I coulda done it. And I woulda too, if I had the chance."

Sally had fallen asleep in her father's lap. She was a wee, sweet thing, with her mother's green eyes and long, dark hair. She was the one Seaver worried about most. The nightmares Farnsworth's brief visit would inspire, blood-drenched dreams she did not deserve.

They wouldn't hear of him leaving without spending one night under their roof. No chicken coop for him. He was shown to a mat Caleb had considerately stuffed with fresh straw, the sheets his mother provided stiff and clean.

In the morning, they sent him on his way with a hearty

breakfast. As he said his farewells and stepped through the doorway, Margaret pressed a thick, wrapped sandwich into his hand, briefly met his eyes, then scurried away.

The boy had seen to his horses and had them ready and waiting.

"Heading north?" Tom Kaline inquired.

"Yellowstone country."

"You heard about that cougar givin' 'em trouble?"

Seaver smiled. "Word gets around."

"I guess they're mighty worked up about it over in Livingston."

"Think there's anything to it?"

Kaline shrugged. "Fella told me it's killed ten men so far. A real man-eater."

"Stories tend to get bigger the more often they're told."

"That's true enough."

"Remember what Mr. Devlin said about that hunter fella, daddy?" Caleb piped up.

"What's that? Oh, yeah. One guy I know said some famous hunter was fixin' to bag the critter. Comin' all the way from back East somewheres. Likely another tall tale."

"Are *you* a hunter, Mr. Thornton?" This from little Sally.

"Not hardly, dearie," Seaver told her. "I don't see much point in killin' something unless you have to."

"Like that mean boy." Tom seemed embarrassed by her directness but her expression was so earnest and forthright, Seaver couldn't help chuckling.

"Yep," he confirmed, "that's exactly right."

Touching the brim of his hat in farewell, Seaver nudged the Nag to get them underway.

"Bye!" Little Sally called after him. "G'bye! G'bye!"

Her voice followed him up the trail, diminishing with

distance. When it was finally gone, its absence was keenly felt.

No attachments and nothing to call his own. That was his lot.

But it doesn't *always* have to be that way, he reminded himself. A man can change, circumstances can change. You never know when something will come along and bump you on to a totally different track. Or, as his daddy liked to say: *Life is what happens when you ain't lookin'.*

As a motto or principle to live by, a person could do a whole lot worse.

CHAPTER FOUR

TOM KALINE WAS RIGHT, Livingston was certainly abuzz over the big cat.

The town had thrived in the two years since its official founding, its success directly attributable to its close proximity to the world's first national park just sixty miles to the south. The Northern Pacific Railroad brought tourists in from the rest of America and had recently completed a branch line from Livingston to the very doorstep of Yellowstone.

News of the "killer cat" was spreading far and wide, thanks to the telegraph wire and newspapers with too many column inches and not enough stories to fill them. As a result, local merchants were up in arms, claiming the cougar was bad for business and might scare people off, cause them to spend their hard-earned vacation dollars elsewhere.

A fund had been taken up among the Livingston business community and a bounty of a thousand dollars offered to anyone who succeeded at ridding the territory of the troublesome feline.

There were those who expressed reservations with the tactic. They suspected a promotional gimmick and wondered at the legality of sponsoring a hunt for an animal located within the confines of what was, after all, a national park and wildlife sanctuary. The park's superintendent prevailed upon his superiors in Washington, who sent a stiffly worded message to Governor Crosby in Helena, demanding the territory make renewed efforts to "protect and preserve" Yellowstone and the animals residing within.

There were veiled hints that if his administration failed to meet its obligations, the U.S. Army might be brought in to enforce park boundaries and police illegal hunting activity.

Most Livingston residents, on the other hand, welcomed the bounty and the furor it created; a sporting atmosphere developed, fuelled by saloon chatter and an active betting pool.

To Seaver, the whole thing seemed ridiculous. No two accounts corroborated each other, "common knowledge" amounting to hearsay and guesswork. *There's more the gravy than the grave to this*, he thought.

He made the rounds, eavesdropping, keeping quiet and taking in as much as he could. One of the local barbershops was, predictably, a hotbed of gossip. The ex-cavalryman who ran it knew only one haircut and was missing all but two fingers on his right hand. But his mouth never stopped moving.

Seaver bought a copy of the local newspaper, the *Enterprise*, and read an editorial strongly endorsing the bounty: "Livingston, after all, is quite literally 'the Gateway City', the primary embarkation point for travelers wishing to visit America's Wonderland, the most unique and exotic locale this vast country of ours has to offer. Surely, no responsible citizen can condemn our city fathers for taking practical steps to protect the lives and livelihood of our people by eradicating this nuisance." The article went on to describe the cat as a "colossus that has survived from pre-history, a relic from a time when humans wore animal skins and dinosaurs roamed the earth".

Heady stuff.

There were several hotels to choose from but he had other resources at his disposal. Margaret Kaline had provided him with the name of a favorite aunt who made her home in Livingston, a widow lady who occasionally let out her extra room to boarders. Seaver located the dwelling on the west side of town with little difficulty and presented its owner, a short, stout woman in her mid-to-late fifties, with the scrap of paper bearing Margaret's hand-printed note.

"You're Mr. Thornton?"

"Yes, ma'am."

"How long are you planning on staying?"

He considered. "Three days. Likely no longer."

"Meals are included, of course. I set a good table."

"I'm happy to pay for your trouble."

"Maggie says something happened out there and that you'll explain."

"I can do that."

She looked him over, finally nodded. "First thing we'll do is get you in a bath." Holding the door open to admit him. She was small and grey-haired but her arms and shoulders looked strong. Likely capable of *carrying* him to the tub, if need be. He liked her already.

"Is the bath extra?"

"It's *compulsory*. One of the conditions for sleeping under my roof. I want to be able to use the sheets again afterward." They both struggled to contain smiles, finally gave up at the same time. "What's your first name, Mr. Thornton?"

"Frank."

"That's a fine name. Strong name. I'm Estelle Montgomery but everyone around here calls me Essie."

"A pleasure, ma'am."

"You took off your hat and cleaned your boots before you came in," she observed shrewdly. "Which means you were brought up right by a woman who made sure you minded your manners."

His grin widened. "Never were truer words spoken. That was mama, all right."

"Where are you from?"

"Oklahoma...but my people originally hail from Texas."

Her eyes lit up. "Well, why didn't you *say* so..."

It turned out that Essie was a native Texan, born and raised near El Paso. Her married name might have been Montgomery but she came from a line that traced itself back to one of the Republic's founding families. "The 'Old Three Hundred', that's what they call us. An aristocracy of sorts. The only ones strong enough to wrest the land from the Mexicans and Comanches. My father and grandfather were both closely acquainted with General Sam Houston. And I don't have to remind you," she added, "down Texas way that name *means* something."

"So how did you end up in Montana?"

She shook her head. "A long, long story. I'd blame it on my husband but he had the bad luck to die of the typhus so he's not around to defend himself."

"Sorry to hear it."

"He was a cattle man, loved wide open spaces and tall skies and so Montana suited him just fine. We came north with twenty-five hundred head and he caught the fever a few days out of Cheyenne. Dead in twenty-four hours. The only one to sicken, no one else getting so much as a sore throat." She looked over, met his gaze. "But we finished the drive." Clearly still proud of the accomplishment. "Brought in every single head and sold 'em at a good price. And I never went home again." He waited but she offered nothing more. She'd said her piece and that was that.

She led him to the parlor, which was festooned with

ceremonial "presentation" swords, faded flags and standards, as well as various armaments dating back a hundred years. It was a shrine to bygone days, bloody times, history writ with the point of a sword or bayonet, punctuated by the cannon's roar. The arsenal of weaponry she'd assembled was impressive and he whistled with appreciation as he took it all in.

"I take it you are well acquainted with firearms, young man."

"I guess you could say that."

She went over to an ornately carved box on the mantle, returned with the finest revolver he'd ever seen. "A Colt Whitneyville-Hartford Dragoon. Silver grips, see? A *pair* of these were presented to my uncle by his fellow officers." She passed him the weapon and scowled as he handled it with exaggerated care. "That's not how you treat a weapon. Show me you know your stuff, Mr. Thornton."

So he did. The pistol weighed over four pounds, the barrel seven-and-a-half inches long. Must have kicked like a mule. First he checked the six-shot cylinder, dry-firing at the floor out of sheer habit. Then he showed off a little, made some passes and draws, finishing with a perfectly executed road agent's spin: holding the gun out to her, upside down and butt first, then deftly reversing it so the butt was back in his hand, the hammer cocked and ready. A stunt originally attributed to "Curly" Bill Brocius.

The entire demonstration took about thirty seconds and at first he thought he'd overdone it. She had backed away and was regarding him with narrowed eyes, her ample rump pressed up against the comforting mass of a heavy armchair.

"I do declare..." Was all she could manage. He thumbed the hammer, releasing it, handed the pistol back to her.

"Beautiful weapon. You clean it regular too, I can tell."

She was open-mouthed, trying to accommodate what she'd just witnessed. "Why, Mr. Thornton," all at once she was beaming at him, reaching out, squeezing his arm. "I do believe I have a gunman under my roof."

It didn't seem politic to lie. "Yes, ma'am, I'm afraid that's so."

She laughed, her face flushed with mischievous pleasure. "Well, son, I can tell you one thing. You sure have come to the right place..."

After showing him his small, neat room, she bade him sit down in the parlor while she fixed him a potent cocktail that tasted of mint and gin. Mainly gin.

"Now let's hear that story Maggie wrote about..."

He told her about her relatives' experiences at the hands of Dwayne Farnsworth, the catastrophe the family had so narrowly escaped. Then he gave her the postscript, describing his own encounter with the kid and his sudden, violent demise.

"Good," Essie Montgomery said. "He only got what was coming to him. So you saw through him, saw him for what he was."

"Guess I have an instinct for bad seeds," he admitted. "And I like to take precautions."

"Quite right." She raised her glass to him. "And now you're here, in our fair town. Which leads me to ask *why*. And I can think of only one obvious answer: our famous cat."

"Mainly I came out of curiosity. Don't think I can put it better than that. Ain't every day you hear about something like that." He polished off the rest of the drink, set it on a nearby table. "I was comin' north anyway. This is what you'd call a detour."

"I just hope you're not wasting your time." Her tone was gruff, dismissive. "The whole thing's a tempest in a teapot. The local chamber of commerce making a big to-do about nothing."

"It's killed men, though nobody seems to know for sure how many."

"That's just it, it's hard to tell what's real and what's pure balderdash."

"Even if it's only one or two—"

"—then compared to our last war, Frank, that cougar is a rank amateur."

"I guess there's that." Conceding the point. She was one sharp lady.

"They're trying to make this wild animal into some kind of supernatural being. Going on about how big it is and how it attacks without warning, a menace on four legs. What utter nonsense."

"'Somethin' out of pre-history', is what I read."

She snorted. "More likely the product of tall tales and too much cheap liquor, if you ask me. Suddenly *everybody's* seeing panthers or knows somebody who's seen one. I don't know why the local business people are complaining—people aren't staying away, they're coming from halfway across the country, hoping to see the thing. They ought to put up a big banner on Main Street, *Welcome to Livingston: Gateway to Cat Country...*"

"So what do you think? Is there really a cat?"

"Oh, it exists all right. In bad dreams, the growling monster lurking just outside the circle of light. Something made from ignorance and fear, the stuff of myth. It exists...but when someone finally gets lucky and kills the poor thing, I doubt it will live up to its inflated reputation. Nor will its demise put an end to the childish terrors that inspired its creation."

Seaver didn't know what to say. In the face of such eloquence he felt slow-witted and inadequate. He watched her refill their glasses. For a long interval they sat facing each other, neither inclined to speak, finding it sufficient to exchange smiles and sip their strong drinks. Already comfortable together, at ease in each other's company.

Like shoes and socks, as his daddy would've said.

In terms of gathering information and learning the lay of the land, he couldn't have asked for a better hostess. His new landlady was well-acquainted with the grand dames of Livingston and occupied a critical place on the grapevine that rushed gossip from one end of town to the other at breakneck speed.

Thus, he learned about some of the local movers and shakers, the politics and personalities that shaped the young community. Livingston was expanding at a dazzling rate and the business people were determined to avoid the boom and bust cycle that often beset western towns. At least three quarters of the population were employed in some capacity by the Northern Pacific Railroad, a fact not lost on anyone. But there was the added benefit of a national park just a short trip down the track. Word of Yellowstone's existence was spreading around the world. The tourists would come by the thousands, perhaps *tens of thousands,* spending money in local shops before boarding the train to Wonderland. The rich and the curious, Americans and foreigners...but perhaps not in as many numbers if there was a ferocious cat prowling about the park. And so the bounty. And the bounty *hunters.*

Much of the activity relating to the cougar seemed to center around the Albemarle Hotel, interested parties gathering there to hear the latest stories and discuss strategy.

"That's where you'll find the Warings, Mister and

Missus."

"Who are they?"

"You've never heard of Philip Waring?"

He frowned. The name *did* seem familiar. "I reckon I have but I can't put my finger on it."

"He's a big game hunter. Writes books too, full of long, gory passages about stalking and killing anything that strikes his fancy. A trail of dead animals stretching from here to Timbuktu. They say he never misses. At least, they *used* to say that..."

"Ma'am?"

"Do you know what irony is, young man?"

"Not to explain it, no, ma'am."

"Irony is when a man known for his steady nerves and above all else his unerring eye, when that man wakes up one morning and, lo and behold, his priceless eyes are failing him, blackness creeping in at the edges."

"Good Lord..."

"No, Frank, I told you, it's *irony* and Philip Waring is *prima facie* evidence of its existence."

"He's *blind*?"

"Not quite but it won't be long. An untreatable condition, I'm told, quite rare. They aren't holding out much hope."

Seaver frowned. "And he's after that cat? In his condition? Man must be loco."

"You don't credit him with some kind of bravery?" He couldn't tell if she was teasing him.

"What does his wife think of such foolishness?"

"Ah," she nodded, toasting his sagacity, "*that* is something the lady in question seems to be keeping to herself..."

After an extended bath and a three-course meal that

left him feeling a trifle bloated, he decided to stretch his legs. Aimed his feet in the direction of downtown Livingston and before long found himself outside the three-story Albemarle, one of a number of red brick buildings present in the commercial district. He entered, passed through the lobby and strode into the saloon.

It was, more correctly, a gentleman's drinking establishment. No raucous piano music or bar chippies with ancient, painted eyes. There was a 40-foot long bar at one end of the room, with the obligatory salty artwork framed behind it. "Venus on the Half-shell". *More like Venus on the heavy side*, Seaver thought. Lots of exposed rolls of flesh. Not a very accomplished rendering, in his opinion. Hardly worth the canvas it was painted on.

It was his intention to remain in the background, an unobtrusive observer, invisible as a wallflower. And that might have been possible under ordinary circumstances. Unfortunately, he happened to wander in just as two men squared off, preparing to stage an old fashioned showdown for the benefit of everyone present.

"Four-eyed freak!" A ginger-bearded giant taunted a bespectacled dude at least a head shorter who, to his credit, didn't seem the slightest bit intimidated by his blustering opponent.

"Your impertinence is insufferable, sir," the offended party snapped. His head was thrust forward, fists clenched at his side. "I daresay you could use a lesson in humility."

The bearded ruffian threw back his head, hollering with affected laughter. "Be damned with you, sir," he returned, mocking the refined delivery of his intended victim. "*I daresay* you're nothing but a Yankee and a greenhorn and gutless to boot."

"I won't take that from the likes of you," the smaller

man bristled.

"C'mon, Hank," a worried looking bartender counseled, "lemme pour you 'nother drink. Whaddaya say?"

The big man ignored him. "I'll send you to hell on a fast horse, you uppity sonofabitch," he snarled at his diminutive adversary.

"Now, you jes' leave the man be! Roosevelt here ain't done nothin' to you, Hank. You're jes' being contrary, is all."

There were murmurs of agreement. Clearly most of those present sided with the Eastern dude and that only served to add fuel to the fire. "To hell with the lot of you. I'm gonna teach this damn pilgrim a lesson he won't forget." Hank wrenched open his coat, exposing an enormous Navy Colt crammed into a leather shoulder holster. "*Pull*, you fancy little twist." But even as he spoke, his hand was darting for the Colt, grabbing for it...and coming up empty.

He raised his head, looked directly into the cool, grey eyes of Frank Seaver. Seaver showed him the big Colt in his hand. He smiled. "Not good enough, *pilgrim*." He twirled the pistol, caught it, cocked it...everyone in the room taking a deep breath. Hank paled, sweat pouring off him like rain. Seaver released the hammer and in one swift, assured movement, stuck the pistol back into its holster. "Let's try that again. This time, with my left hand. Go ahead." Hank stared at him, his brain working hard to process what was happening.

Something gave him away, a tremor, or maybe his eyes changed. In the next *instant*, the Colt was in Seaver's left hand, cocked, pointed at Hank's adam's apple. "Whoops, careful there, friend." He released the hammer, returned the Colt to its scabbard, flipping the man's coat over it disdainfully. "I'm a touch slower with my left," he explained to Hank, who looked like he'd been gut shot, pale as a hungry ghost. "You can probably tell." Giving him the Stare. "You wanna see that trick again?"

Instead of answering, Hank started backing up, stumbling over a chair as he navigated unsteadily toward the door, jeers and catcalls following him out.

Seaver quickly found himself surrounded by the other denizens of the bar, each of them anxious to congratulate him and fill his hand with a drink. However, if he expected gratitude from the one called Roosevelt, he was sorely mistaken.

"Bloody interloper," he barked, when Seaver offered him his hand. "Made me look like a greenhorn." His teeth were square and straight and white, his fringed, buckskin outfit, on closer inspection, custom made and of the finest quality. No mere cowpoke, possessing the pride and temperament of a man used to being obeyed. Despite the protestations of those around him, he would not be mollified and left in high dudgeon.

Seaver was bewildered by his behavior but Pete, the man tending bar, told him to forget it. "Don't mind him. He's a bit of a hothead. Some of us think he's got some kinda death wish. He's an Eastern yokel, as you can probably tell, but we don't hold it agin him. He's tough as nails. Don't get on his wrong side or you'll find that out for yourself!" Seaver shrugged, indicating it was of little matter to him. The bartender steered another drink his way. "On the house," he explained. "T.R.'s got a lot of friends here...and that was one sweet move you pulled on ol' Hank. Sure took nerve, I'll tell you that.."

"First time I ever tried it," Seaver lied. "Just got lucky is all."

But he could tell the wily barkeeper didn't believe him.

◆ ◆ ◆

The next morning, after a substantial breakfast, Essie Montgomery joined him at the dining room table, bringing along a fresh pot of coffee.

Their conversation was light, breezy; a maiden aunt entertaining a visiting nephew. But she had something on her mind and finally got down to it.

"Do you mind if I look at your hands, Frank?" He hesitated, then held them out to her. She leaned forward, gripping his fingers, making a minute examination. Her hands were short and blunt, roughened by decades of honest work. "They aren't very big, are they? Still, I bet they're fast. Fast enough to catch flies." He smiled, not denying it. "My brother Cal was a pistoleer," she confided, looking across at him. "He was killed a month before his twenty-third birthday."

"Sorry to hear it."

Her eyes were tracking back in time. "A beautiful, beautiful boy. Wild and ungovernable." Her next words raised the hairs on the back of his neck. "One day he went up against a man much like you. Older, more experienced. He was shot down in the street. Some place I never heard of in Kansas. He's buried there, in a pauper's grave. We never heard about it for three months." She refilled their cups while he struggled vainly for something to contribute. "How old are you, Frank?" Catching him off guard again.

"Thirty-seven or thereabouts."

"You're a survivor then."

"Or just plain lucky."

"And your name is *not* Thornton." He stared at her but she was undeterred. "If you've lived this long it means you know your way around guns *and* you've done your fair share of killing. Such a man doesn't go unnoticed. There are people who follow the careers and accomplishments of men like you. Me, for instance. Just because I'm a woman doesn't mean I can't have an avid interest in violence. I am a student of it—like my dear brother, I suspect it is in my blood. I'll wager if you told me your name, your *real* name, I'd recognize it. I feel like I should know who you are..." Her expression thoughtful as she pondered possible candidates.

He was buffaloed. "I...believe you have me at a disadvantage, ma'am." Withdrawing his hands and settling back in the chair.

"Come, come, my boy. No need to be coy. I subscribe to a number of newspapers in the region and friends throughout the country send me clippings. Let's see...you're not old enough to be Clay Allison and as far as I know he's still down in Texas. Jim Courtright? Joe Kidd? I don't see the resemblance." She saw his face, chuckled. "All right, all right, have it your way. You're a cool customer, Frank Thornton. I may be privy to everybody else's business in this town but I also have the good sense to know when to mind my own. And I want you to know you're welcome to stay here as long as you like. In the meantime, I'll keep my eye out for folks inquiring into your affairs. How does that sound?" Reaching for her china cup, one with her favorite floral pattern.

He pondered her words, then extended his hand once again. "The name's Seaver, ma'am. Frank Seaver."

The cup slipped from her fingers, the force of the impact splitting the saucer in two, ruining a perfect set.

Essie was finishing the dusting when someone knocked on the front door. She found Seaver in the parlor, reading a copy of *Moll Flanders* he'd found on a nearby shelf. "It was a messenger from the hotel." She held out a small white card.

Philip Waring.

On the reverse, hand-printed: *Albemarle Hotel, 2:00 p.m. (Rm.12)*

"Man of few words."

"Most likely his wife wrote it. She handles most of his affairs now. Poor devil would be lost without her, I imagine."

"You didn't sound nearly so sympathetic yesterday."

"I disapprove of his chosen vocation. I believe killing for pleasure or sport is revolting. But I concede the man has a formidable reputation. He is, by all accounts, courageous and ruthlessly professional. He's hunted all over the world, you know, faced down charging elephants and voracious tigers without batting an eye. Expert marksman too...at least he used to be."

"Going blind like that—"

"A terrible thing. Apparently, he can make out people, objects if they're close enough. But each day more and more detail is lost. The shadows closing in."

"Sounds like a nightmare."

"I hear it is not a cross he bears well." He glanced up from the card. "He drinks. To excess. Becomes boastful, sometimes abusive."

"Losing his sight and a drunk on top of it. I don't like his chances of collecting that bounty."

"And he's not the only one after it. There are plenty of others, some of them with more black powder than common sense. And they usually end up getting lost, stumbling back into town, more dead than alive. *Hunters!*" Pouring as much scorn as possible into the word.

"Met a fella in the bar. Stocky, little round glasses. Came from out East originally. Name of Roosevelt."

She nodded. "That would be Theodore Roosevelt. Has a

spread over in the Dakota Territory. Word is that he lost his whole family to influenza. So he pulled up stakes and moved west. Now he's living next to nowhere and playing at being a cattleman."

"Feisty, I'll give him that."

"He's another one after the cat. Has his own party, cowboys, by the sound of it. No tenderfeet. I'd rate his chances higher than most. But that's rough country and you never know what it's liable to throw at you."

"I reckon I still don't see what the fuss is all about," he confessed. "Like the man said, it's all sound and fury. Far as I can tell, it don't amount to much more than a hill of horse manure."

"Ah, but you're not seeing the big picture. This isn't just any cougar, Frank. This animal represents savage, untamed nature. It must be captured and put on display or, better yet, killed outright. To allow it to roam free, king of its domain, why, that would be a crime against progress."

He was shaking his head. "You sure have a way of looking at the world, Essie." Making it plain he was praising her.

"The poor thing is a victim of the future," she concluded sadly, "the terrible, unstoppable future. And so are we all. Only most of us haven't figured it out yet."

CHAPTER FIVE

EN ROUTE TO THE Albemarle, Seaver was waylaid by the town sheriff.

The lawman's gut arrived about a second ahead of the rest of him. He had to keep his gun belt cinched high, above his belly button, because, like most men sporting that configuration, his hips were practically nonexistent. *Nothing grows in the shade*, Seaver thought unkindly, watching as the fat man came huffing up to him. He was perspiring like a cold bottle, his face beet red.

"You're Thornton, is that right?" He kept his badge highly polished even if the rest of him was a sight for sore eyes.

"That's right, sheriff."

"Name's Van Dyke, Roscoe Van Dyke. Put 'er there." His hand was soft and damp. "Been meanin' to make your acquaintance. Mind if I walk with you a ways?"

"Just headin' over to the hotel."

"Well, there you go. So am I." He waddled along beside Seaver, finding it difficult to keep up with the taller man's long strides. "Heard about the commotion with Hank Sears. You're the talk of the town. Pretty slick move."

Seaver kept his eyes straight ahead. "If you say so."

"Not just me, everyone who was there. And a good many that weren't. Takes a lot of nerve to pull a stunt like that. Not many could manage it." They had reached the hotel, faced each other a few yards from the front entrance. "*Thornton*...any reason I should be familiar with that name?"

"None I can think of." Seaver's patience with the man was wearing thin. "I got no particular claim to fame."

"Is that so? Where you from, you don't mind my askin'?"

"Oklahoma, but I been just about everywhere. Last few years it was Kansas. Had me a little spread but...things didn't work out. Ended up leavin' the place to my brother."

Van Dyke grunted. "Thought you might be from Missouri or thereabouts. Could be I heard that somewhere." Giving him a sly look.

Seaver countered with the Stare. "I doubt it. Been awhile since I was back that way. Don't hardly recollect the place any more."

"Plannin' on stayin' in town long?" The sheriff laced his chubby fingers over his belly, enjoying himself.

"I doubt it. Just passin' through."

"What's your—"

"Mr. Thornton." It was more a statement of fact than a question. Seaver and the sheriff turned toward a negro man waiting by the door. He was over six feet tall and looked strong enough to pull a train, never mind his receding hairline and graying temples. His left arm hung awkwardly and there was a patch of scar tissue visible on his throat, only partially covered by the collar of the blue linen shirt he wore.

The sheriff scowled at him. "You say something, boy?"

The black man's face gave nothing back, impassive, inured to insult. "Mr. Waring instructed me to meet Mr. Thornton here." To Seaver: "You're right on time, sir." He barely acknowledged Van Dyke and that nettled the fat man.

"I guess this nigger has business with you. I'll be seeing you, Thornton." Off he went, clumping down the wooden sidewalk, people darting out of his path, giving him plenty of room.

"I do believe he's as wide as he is tall," Seaver observed, but the other man acted like he hadn't heard.

"Mr. Waring's waiting inside. Room twelve."

"I got the card." He stepped up beside the black man but neither of them seemed inclined to shake hands. Waring's emissary cut an impressive figure, boasting a solid physique, exceedingly well-preserved despite his obvious injuries.

"The name's Caliban." Noting Seaver's reaction. "You know Shakespeare?"

"Some. *The Tempest* was the last thing he done, wasn't it?"

"So they say. I chose the name myself. After all, doesn't Prospero call Caliban a 'thing of darkness'?"

"I seem to recall a line to that effect."

"Like every master, Prospero thinks his slave should be grateful to him."

"Seems to me Caliban ain't no paragon of virtue either."

"He has his reasons." Caliban's face hardened. "At least he's not a willing servant. He *hates* Prospero. I respect that. It's why I took his name. Why I'll no longer answer to my slave name. No one will ever call me *that* again. I burned it the same night I burned my clothes, my past, everything. A new name for a new, free man." Seaver nodded. "You'd best be heading up. Mr. Waring doesn't like to be kept waiting."

"His wife there too?"

"I suppose so. She's usually with him now. Ever since..."

"I heard about it. Tough luck."

"There are worse things, I guess."

"Off hand, I can't think of many."

"He doesn't want your pity, that's the first thing you should know. And he can be hard on people. Got a temper too. So stay on your toes. Just a little friendly advice."

Seaver's curiosity got the better of him. "Mind if I ask about those scars? Were they in the line of duty or—"

But the dark man didn't let him finish. "I'll be seeing you around." He started away.

"A lion do that?" Seaver called after him. But Caliban neither slowed nor offered any reply.

Seaver knocked and a male voice answered from within. He pushed open the door to room twelve and entered.

There was a bottle on the nightstand beside the bed. Kentucky bourbon, good stuff.

It was the *second* thing that caught his eye.

Just as he stepped inside, Patricia Waring bustled into her husband's chamber through a connecting door. Their simultaneous arrival surprised them both. She was a beautiful woman, that much was immediately apparent. Pale, oval face, lightly freckled, with prominent cheekbones. Her simple outfit became her: high-collared, cream blouse, brown, ankle-length skirt. He realized he was staring, dragged his eyes away, feeling thoroughly abashed and discomposed.

"Impeccable timing," someone commented and they turned toward the speaker.

The bourbon was placed within easy reach of the man on the bed. Philip Waring was propped up on two pillows, his shirt untucked, collar open at his throat. Caught in repose. He had an overlarge head and unruly thatch of sandy brown hair. Broad-shouldered, thick-framed. Fit at one time, now declining into flab. A cloth was draped over his eyes but he removed it to greet his visitors. His gaze was direct but lacked focus, aimed at some point between them. A vague, general glance that took in everything and nothing.

"Darling," his wife spoke up. "I believe it's Mr. Thornton, the man you sent for."

"Frank Thornton, ma'am. Pleased to make your acquaintance, Mr. Waring." He'd removed his hat prior to entering, held it at his side.

"We don't stand on ceremony around here, do we, Pat?" Her smile was thin, tired. Waring swung his feet to the floor and rose, extending his hand. "Pleased to meet you, Frank. I'm Philip Waring and this is my wife, Patricia."

Seaver gave a quick nod to the woman, then moved to intercept the proffered hand. Waring's grip was firm, well-practiced. "Pleasure, sir."

"Grab us a couple of glasses, will you, Pat?" She moved to obey and, meanwhile, Waring gestured in the direction of the room's only chair. "Have a seat. The accommodations are somewhat primitive but at least the furniture is sturdy. *That* I can vouch for." Seaver seated himself while Waring perched on the edge of the bed. He continued his surreptitious examination of his host, noting that while his vision might be impaired, he retained considerable energy and vitality.

Formidable was the first word that came to mind. Not physically a huge man but thick and powerful. Radiating confidence, presenting the assured mien of a born leader. In his prime, Waring had probably been a forceful, dynamic figure, the kind of man you'd want in charge of an expedition into *terra incognita*. Fearless, unruffled by misfortune or accident, achieving the impossible thanks to resilience of mind and indomitable will.

They were an exotic couple and Seaver wondered what

they thought of Livingston's finest accommodations. The room was tidy but small and scantily furnished. A washstand, dresser, the iron, four-poster bed and not much more. The window was shut and covered, the noises from the street below muted.

There was no scattering of clothes or casual sloppiness. Everything in its proper place. A room suited to a blind man, he realized, well thought out, right down to the placement of the round-keyed typewriter, which was centered on a square, wooden table set against the wall, a ream of plain, unlined paper stacked beside it. On top of that, a single book, the spine facing toward him: *The Sportsman's Handbook of Practical Collecting and Preserving Trophies*. Not exactly thrilling reading...

Patricia came in with two glasses, poured them each a drink. Waring accepted a glass, then leaned forward. "I'm sure you're more than a little curious why I asked to meet you, Frank." Once she'd given them their drinks, Patricia seemed content to fade into the background, ceding attention to her husband. An admirable woman. "We're both strangers in Livingston, fish out of water in many respects. I don't know what brought you here but I suspect you might have an inkling as to my intentions." He waited but Seaver didn't take his cue. His silence seemed to bother Waring, who glanced at his wife before continuing. "Am I correct or..."

"I know who you are." As he spoke, he noticed Waring adjust his gaze a fraction, compensating for the location of his voice.

"Then I reckon you know why I'm here."

"I suppose so." They both took a drink, considering each other, making rapid assessments.

"And what is your view of such an endeavor?"

Ah, Seaver thought, now we get to the meat of the matter. "I'd say...I think that a half-blind man hunting a dangerous cat seems to me to be a damn fool proposition. The country in these parts is rough, even on someone...well, someone who ain't in your condition. That's blunt talk but there it is. Take it or leave it."

No one said anything. To his right, Seaver could hear Patricia Waring breathing. He finished the liquor in his glass, waiting for what happened next.

"You certainly don't pull any punches, do you?" Waring's voice sounded strained but still civil.

"Just tellin' it the way I see it."

"Well, let me tell *you* something, Frank. Under ordinary circumstances, I'd be in complete agreement with you. The Yellowstone is no place for someone operating under any kind of handicap. But I'm no ordinary man." He drank what was in his glass and held it out for a refill. Patricia obliged, but when she looked at Seaver, he shook his head. "I very much wish we could have met a few years ago. Before...this." He made a vague gesture toward his face. "My eyesight was unbelievably sharp. I *saw* things, the smallest objects, in precise detail. Even in the midst of a hunt—a rhino in full charge, plowing through the sawgrass toward me, a puma leaping for my throat—I was aware of *everything*, right down to a blue rivulet of vein, a sprinkle of mud or a broken tooth. Have you ever experienced something like that?"

"I...think I know what you mean," Seaver conceded, offering no further elaboration.

"*Of course* you do." Waring gestured with his free hand, eager, excited, his failing eyes still managing to convey great reservoirs of passion. "Certain men are imbued with a gift. A coolness under fire. Others might lose their heads and panic but our kind doesn't. We are calm, collected, welcoming any challenge, refusing every setback." He paused to take a good-sized belt. "Patricia, I believe Mr. Thornton's glass is empty."

"I'm fine."

"I'll have a little more. Just a splash." She poured and backed away. "Now...where was I? Ah. Yes, as I was saying, I sense we're birds of a feather, you and I, sharing many of the same ideals and values. I hope you don't think that presumptuous of me, but I have an instinct about such things, don't I, Pat?"

"Yes, dear."

"You're quite right: I *am* going blind. In six months, a year at most..." Barely missing a beat: "But you'd be absolutely *wrong* if you think I'm helpless. Far from it, I assure you. My eyes may be going, Frank, but my other senses have compensated for my condition, become sharper, highly attuned. My hearing, for example, is remarkably acute. I can detect insect wings brushing together, the most distant or minute sound. And there's something else, something I feel quite confident confessing to a man such as yourself." He paused and Seaver wondered what was coming next. "I'm talking about a faculty far removed from ordinary human experience. An ability to anticipate a threat or impending danger with unnatural accuracy. I *know* when something is going to happen before it happens. Pat has witnessed this gift, so has my associate Caliban. They will both testify to the truthfulness of my claim."

"My husband isn't exaggerating, Mr. Thornton," Patricia Waring confirmed. "I've seen it for myself. It is...uncanny."

"I may not have perfect sight but I retain all my instincts and abilities, as well as some new ones I hadn't previously known existed. I believe that despite my condition I am still Philip Waring. Not the man I was but, then again, perhaps something *more*."

Seaver shifted in his chair. "That may be so, Mister—Philip. But I still don't see where I—"

"Of course!" The famed hunter cried, leaping to his feet. "Now we get to the *real* reason I brought you here today. And it's simply this: I want you to accompany me on our little expedition into Yellowstone Park. With the help of a local guide, our party shall proceed to the last known location of the cougar and begin the hunt from there. I propose to stalk it, corner it and kill it. That's my plan, in a nutshell."

Seaver was taken aback, at once intrigued and wary. "Accompany you...but what would I be doin'?" He glanced at Patricia but all her attention was focused on her husband. Had he discussed this with her prior to making the offer?

"Your role is to provide extra security against anything untoward we might encounter on the trail. This is hostile terrain and, as you've probably heard, there are still Indians about. I have it on good authority that some of our red-skinned friends have taken a ridiculously proprietary view toward the cat. They believe it to be some kind of spirit animal, perhaps even the manifestation of one of their ancestors or some such rot. If it truly *is* a supernatural creature, their worries are entirely unfounded—my bullets will merely pass right through it. So...now you know my thoughts. What do you say?" The Warings waited while he mulled over the offer.

"Would I be participatin' in the hunt...or am I only along as an extra gun?"

Waring sat down on the bed again, hands on his knees, his expression earnest. "I hadn't given it much thought but, yes, of course you're welcome to join in the game. Are you a sporting man, Frank?"

"Not really. I'm more interested as a spectator." Waring's relief was so palpable he couldn't risk a dig. "Personally, I got no reason to go up against your mountain lion. He ain't botherin' me so I'd just as soon leave him be."

"You don't have any moral qualms against killing the brute, do you?" A hint of worry crept into Waring's voice.

"No. If he came after me, I'd do what was necessary to protect myself, same as anybody else."

"I understand. And I appreciate your candor." Waring slapped his knees. "Well, Frank, am I wrong or do I detect some interest in my humble proposal?"

"It would involve changing my plans. I'd like to think about it, if you don't mind."

"Of course. But, to be honest, I do feel certain time constraints. I'd like to leave Livingston as soon as it's feasible. I fear if we wait too long, some other enterprising soul will steal our prize *and* the accompanying laurels." He chuckled, then winced, reaching for his eyes. His wife frowned and moved toward him but he waved her away brusquely and she subsided. "These damned peepers of mine," Waring complained.

"You should rest, dear," his wife said. "Dr. Schultz was quite insistent—"

"Yes, yes," he replied, clearly weary of the refrain. "You're right. See Frank out, will you, dear? He mustn't think us uncivilized."

"No worry of that." He stood. "Good day to you, sir."

"Please, Frank, it's Philip. Or Phil, once you get to know me better. And I hope you will." They shook hands again. "Thanks for stopping by. I heard about what happened downstairs and wanted to meet someone who can out-draw a man for his own gun." He chuckled. "My compliments." He went to drink but his glass was empty.

"Don't believe everything you hear." Seaver stood at the door. "People embellish things."

"Ah, but what you did makes for grand storytelling, Frank," Waring remarked, lying back on the bed, "and you come out of it looking very fine indeed."

Patricia Waring accompanied him into the hallway. They passed the atrium with its leaded glass skylight and Seaver found himself wishing they could go in and tarry awhile, sit and talk of matters of far more importance than this ridiculous hunt.

They stood at the top of the stairs. Distorted voices floated up from the lobby and they could hear shouts of laughter and a hum of activity originating from the bar off to the right. She seemed distracted, ill at ease. He felt completely out of his element. It had been a long time since he'd been at close quarters with such an attractive woman. She was different from any female he was likely to meet. Cultivated and decent. He didn't know how to conduct himself, what to do with his hands.

She was in her late twenties, her auburn hair falling in ringlets, framing the loveliest eyes he'd ever seen. He felt foolish and clumsy in her presence. All at once he was anxious to take his leave of her before he embarrassed or offended her with an ill-considered remark. He was about to say a quick "adios" and make his escape, when she reached out with one of her small, white hands, forestalling him.

"My husband is a great man, Mr. Thornton. Not was, *is*. His affliction casts a pall over his future but he's strong, like a bull. He simply *won't* allow it to defeat him."

"Ma'am, I respect your devotion to your man, it speaks

well of you. But...he's a *hunter*." He struggled for the right words, gave up and blundered on. "This isn't a club foot or missing fingers. He calls it a handicap but surely it's more than that."

"I understand your misgivings but, forgive me, if you knew him better you would realize how mistaken you are." She removed her hand and he immediately missed her touch. "I hope I haven't offended you. And I hope you will give serious consideration to joining us. I can tell Philip likes you and it would be a relief having you along. He's convinced that you're just the man we'll need if we find ourselves in a tight spot. I think he's right."

"I still don't understand what he expects of me."

"You're *not* hired help and he doesn't require a caretaker. Be his companion, his confidante. I think he needs that right now." Her lips trembled. "He admires you, a man's man. Someone he can relate to, who isn't intimidated by his fierceness or unafraid to tell him what he needs to hear, even if..."

"...he doesn't want to hear it," he finished for her.

"Yes. Yes, that's it exactly. You don't back down or allow yourself to be browbeaten. He likes that. He might even listen to you, certainly more than..." Leaving the rest of it unsaid.

"I don't know about that. If he's willing to face down a charging elephant, I don't expect he'd pay much heed to the likes of me. Besides, what about his man Caliban? He's been around a lot longer, surely he has some influence."

She shook her head. "Until not long ago I might have agreed with you. But Cal is getting older and has become quite...quarrelsome. Especially after he was mauled by a black bear last year. It happened in northern Michigan, the upper peninsula. We had no inkling there was a bear in the area. We were fishing and it must have been attracted to our catch. It went for Cal and my husband..." She sighed. "For the first time I can remember he aimed and *missed*. First time in all the years I've known him. I suspect it was his eyes, the beginning of...he denied it but I think that was at least partially responsible. Cal didn't blame him, of course..."

"You sure of that?"

She shook her head. "He's like family. He was with my husband even before I met him. They've traveled the world together. After Philip, he is undoubtedly the most fearless man I know. And the best." She brought her fingers to her lips, stopping the flood of words. "I've probably told you far more than you need to know about our affairs. But I wanted to make you aware of who we are and the circumstances that brought us here. Now I'll leave you and return to my husband." Holding out her hand. "I hope to see you again. Good day, Mr. Thornton."

He watched her proceed down the hallway, back toward their rooms. He was still holding his hat. He crammed it onto his head and started the descent to the main floor, preoccupied and distracted, oblivious to his immediate surroundings.

Philip Waring had made a definite impression, no question, but it was his *wife* who dominated Frank Seaver's thoughts. The pressure of her small, thin hand, her fetching, almond-colored eyes.

He had never been a man ruled by his passions. Indeed, his longevity was directly related to his presence of mind and relative equanimity. But Patricia Waring affected him in strange, unaccountable ways. She attracted and fascinated him, a woman unique to his experience and if he hadn't fallen for her already, it was only a matter of time.

He knew it was a dangerous and ridiculous predicament for a man of his age and history to get involved in, but was equally certain it couldn't be helped.

A woman will turn a proud man to butter and a genius into a simpleton, as his daddy liked to say.

But never, young Frank noticed, within earshot of his wife.

CHAPTER SIX

THAT NIGHT, AFTER ANOTHER of Essie's belly-stretching meals, Frank Seaver went for a leisurely amble around Livingston.

It was hard to believe that two years ago the place had been little more than a cluster of tents by the river. Then the railroad passed through, bringing with it coach loads of tourists and curiosity seekers bound for the park, established ten years previously. It was a fortuitous series of events and the town was certainly flourishing at present...but who knew how long it would last.

Livingston spread out along the valley floor south of (and perpendicular to) the tracks. Much of the land to the north had been claimed by the Northern Pacific Railroad and earmarked for a gigantic roundhouse, extensive machine shops and stockyards.

The residential neighborhoods varied in terms of affluence and ostentation but were uniformly barren of trees. The streets were wide and dusty and new construction was in evidence everywhere. There was a substantial Chinese community, their presence yet another byproduct of the railroad.

The commercial district was situated directly across from the train station. It consisted, mainly, of rows of two and three story red brick establishments that appeared to be doing good trade: Bank of Livingston, Saxe and Fryer's News & Fruits, Merchants' Hotel, Babcock & Miles...

Eventually he wound up back at the Albemarle, though

he had no particular reason for stopping there. Was he hoping to cross paths with Philip Waring...or his charming wife?

There was a spirited poker game in progress in the far corner, a well-heeled crowd playing for higher stakes than he could afford. The air was dense with cigar smoke and the game seemed to be on the square. He was tempted to pull up a chair but unwilling to risk any portion of his stake. Not until he'd figured out this business with the Warings. He left them to it.

A boisterous group lined the bar, some he recognized from the previous day. A considerable proportion of those present were making regular use of the wide-mouthed, metal spittoons placed at strategic intervals on the floor. Their accuracy was unerring.

Philip Waring was holding court and his attentive circle of listeners included Sheriff Van Dyke and Theodore Roosevelt. The rest of the group was made up of a mix of locals and some hard-looking seeds who looked like they'd just ridden into town. They were caked with trail dust and smelled of the range. Shabby clothing, snarled hair, unkempt beards.

And compare that to Roosevelt, who stood out from everyone else with his spectacles, round, sombrero-like hat and custom-made duds. He looked clean cut, strait-laced and unimposing, which was probably what had drawn the ire of Hank and, undoubtedly, others like him. But Roosevelt wasn't a man to back down from a challenge and exhibited no fear when the going got tough. He might seem soft and pampered but he was all grit inside, where it mattered most.

"—had my stout companion Caliban in its terrible jaws but, gentlemen, quicker than you can say 'ready, aim, fire!', I dispatched the savage beast with a single, perfectly aimed shot in the brain. Thus saving a valuable member of my party, while preserving the integrity of the hide. Which, I might add, adorns my drawing room back home in Baltimore as we speak." His audience laughed appreciatively, raising their glasses to him. The famed hunter rewarded their approval by banging his hand on the oak bar top, demanding another round for his "well met companions".

Seaver sidled up, caught Pete the barkeep's eye, signaled for a beer. Paying with his own coin, not including himself in Waring's party. He received his drink first and turned to survey the room. Out of habit, he had positioned himself so that he had excellent sightlines. Not taking any chances. Remembering the back-shooting bastards who murdered Hickok and Jesse.

Sheriff Van Dyke tipped him a nod, as did the burly fellow next to him, who reminded Seaver of an old time mountain man. He wore a rough leather tunic and bearclaw necklace. Thickset, his beard nearly chest-length, shot through with grey-white hair.

"Extraordinary," Theodore Roosevelt commented, in response to Waring's latest anecdote. He regarded the hunter with open admiration. "What a life you have led! Adventurous, thrilling...truly the stuff of legend!"

Waring basked in his praise. He was quite drunk, swollen with self-importance. "It's true," he conceded, "I have seen things that beggar description. My books, *bah*, they barely scratch the surface! How can mere words convey what it's like to see the veldt at dawn, the mists rising like a heavenly host? The vast savannah of southern Africa, which contains every variety of creature you can imagine...and some that truly defy belief. Those are sights you can't possibly..." He faltered. "Come, then, gentlemen, drink up! To your health!"

They toasted him right back and Waring poured the whiskey down, immediately signaling for more. One of them must have said something to him because he turned toward Seaver, holding up his hands as if making an announcement. "Ah! What's this? Mr. Thornton has decided to join us. Perhaps he'll amuse us with more of his sleight of hand, eh?" The men around him chuckled, while darting nervous glances Seaver's way. "No? Well, then maybe he'll allow me to buy him a drink." He snapped his fingers to place the order.

"That's okay. I've already got one."

Waring shrugged, as if it was of little consequence to him but Seaver could see he was nettled. The hunter was momentarily distracted when Pete asked him to settle up for the round. Seaver looked away and spotted Roosevelt bearing down on him.

"I wanted a word with you, Thornton," he said, keeping his voice low. He appeared discomfited and at first Seaver thought he was working up the nerve to issue some kind of challenge. But it turned out Roosevelt had something else in mind. "I merely wish to say that, upon further reflection, I realize I acted with little couth the other day and I wanted to say...that is..."

"I shouldn't have interfered," Seaver stated. "You were the injured party and you had every right to stand up for yourself. The fault was mine, sir." He held out his hand. "Shall we let bygones be bygones?"

Roosevelt beamed at him, his eyes, magnified by the spectacles, sparkling with pleasure. Flashing those big, square teeth again. "A capital response, Mr. Thornton! Roosevelt's the name and I am a man who appreciates a gallant gesture. It is a pleasure to make your acquaintance." He pumped Seaver's hand vigorously. A small, strong hand, calloused and knobby from hard work.

Waring had commenced another colorful anecdote, this one about a buffalo that had charged from a concealing thicket, barely leaving him time to bring his trusty rifle to his shoulder and—

The story was a good one and Waring an excellent raconteur, despite his advanced state of intoxication. Just as the account reached its thrilling, if inevitable, climax, Seaver happened to glance toward the door and spotted Patricia peering inside. He pushed away from the bar, doffing his hat as he approached her.

She appeared to take scant notice of his civility. Her face was creased with worry and she kept sneaking looks past him, her attention focused on her husband.

"Can I be of assistance, ma'am?"

Her smile was forced, artificial. The room was smoky and smelled of liquor and unwashed men. No place for a woman of her quality. "I just wanted to make sure...I was hoping I wouldn't find him like this." Her eyes sought his. "Please don't think less of him, Mr. Thornton. What you're seeing, the way he is now..." She sighed. "It's difficult to explain."

"I think I understand."

She regarded him with those brown, solemn eyes and for the first time he didn't look away, returning her gaze. "Do you? Do you really?"

"A man like that is hard on himself and he's even harder on the people around him. He can't help wantin' the life he used to have, the things his mind insists he's still capable of even if his body won't let him have his way." The speech surprised them both but he wasn't done. "There's a lot of anger inside him. Pain too, I suppose. But it's the anger that's worst. Eatin' him up, lookin' for something or someone to blame."

Her head dipped in acknowledgment. "Perhaps you *do* understand after all."

"It's a tough situation for a man to come to grips with. I feel bad for him. Not bein' able to see the beautiful things right in front of him."

She got his meaning, dipped her eyes modestly. "Yes. He retains all the passion for his old life: the love of the hunt, the satisfaction of a good, clean kill. It's still there, inside him."

"But he's going *blind*, Patricia. Sooner or later he's going to have to either come to terms with that or..."

He saw that she was crying. "Yes. I *know*. And I'm terrified when I think about what it's doing to him."

"Forgive the unkindness, ma'am, but I can't help wonderin' what he's doin' here. What does he hope to prove? Even if he manages to find the cat, he won't be able to draw a bead or know for sure—"

"Caliban—"

"—can't do nothin' but point and holler directions. What good is that when you got an angry mountain lion bearin' down on you and—" But he couldn't continue. Her face was wet with tears, her expression anguished. She broke away, fleeing toward the stairs. Seaver could only stand there and stare after her. Not for the first time bemoaning his complete lack of tact.

He turned back, sensing at once that Philip Waring was watching him from over by the bar. His eyes were supposed to be shot, yet at that moment Waring was staring *right at him*. Then Seaver remembered the boasts he'd made regarding the sharpness of his remaining senses. Had he heard their exchange, even through the clamor and background din?

"Mr. Thornton?"

Two of the gamblers had left the table and were now bracketing him. They were dressed like successful gents, tailored suits, expensive hats, boots shined to a gloss. Men of substance, their raiments stated, men who did serious work and sought high station.

"Help you, gentlemen?"

"I'm Arch Foley and this is my associate, Ed Bauer. We've, ah, been wanting to meet you." They seemed relieved that he wasn't averse to shaking their soft, smooth hands. "We'd like a moment of your time, if you're agreeable." They indicated a nearby empty table, where the three of them were soon seated. "Can I get you anything?"

"A fresh beer would be nice."

Foley waved at the bartender, holding up three fingers. "Consider it done."

"Appreciate it." Returning to his taciturn ways now that Patricia Waring was out of the picture. The drinks arrived within moments, sneaky Pete slipping him a wink. *Watch these two jaspers...*

"Mr. Thornton, we'd like to put a proposal to you which I hope you will at least entertain."

"No harm in listenin'."

Foley was the one doing all the talking, his companion content to sit back and ride along on his coat tails. "We like the cut of your jib, sir, if you don't mind my speaking so directly. You certainly create an impression when you walk into a room. This town needs a man like that, someone who inspires respect and trust among its law-abiding citizens and strikes fear into, well, those who aren't so inclined to live by the law, if you get my meaning."

Seaver raised the mug to hide his smile. It was a pitch he'd heard before and he had a pretty good idea where it was leading. But before he could head them off at the pass, Ed Bauer decided to add his two cents' worth. "Livingston is a growing community, Frank. A community with a prosperous future, under the right circumstances. We are, in every sense of the word, at a crossroads. The gateway to the northwest. Lewis and Clark blazed a trail through here nearly a century ago and immediately recognized the potential of this region." He glanced over at his colleague, relinquishing the floor.

"But in order for us to achieve that potential, we *must* have rule of law. Certain recent events have made it clear that our sheriff lacks the, ah, shall we say intestinal fortitude required for the position." Foley's fingernails were clean and trimmed; his right hand bore a ring with a large blue stone. His watch was hooked to his vest with a gold chain and hasp. "We need a new man and we're dead certain you're the one we're looking for."

"We are prepared to offer a generous salary to a particularly attractive candidate," Bauer added. "Well above the going rate. And speaking on behalf of the local business community, I can promise you our full support for any tactics, however unpleasant, you might find necessary to employ to keep our streets safe."

Seaver pretended to mull over their offer. He tipped up his glass, drained its contents. As he set it down, his eyes happened to fall on the portly figure of Livingston's current serving sheriff, who was viewing their discussion with an expression of bewildered hurt. "You boys lookin' for a sheriff or a hired gun?"

"Whatever it takes." Foley's indifference was downright chilling. "A peaceful town is a prosperous town." He produced cigars, offering them around. They lit up, inhaled appreciatively.

"What do you say, Frank?" Bauer pressed him. "Interested?"

"Shall we settle terms?" Foley, eager to close the deal.

Seaver sat back, blowing a plume of smoke toward the high ceiling. "I admit, it's a tempting offer. But I gotta turn it down." Their faces dropped into their beer mugs. "Someone's beaten you to the punch. Mr. Waring over there hired me to ride shotgun for him and it sounds like we'll be leavin' in the next day or two."

They glanced at each other, disappointed that their scheme had fallen through. "Indeed," Arch Foley remarked, "that is unfortunate." He brightened. "Surely, however, that will be a relatively short-lived assignment. Once you're finished, you could return to Livingston and—"

"Sorry, boys." He rose, cigar hooked in the corner of his mouth. "I got plans and they don't involve wearin' a badge. Besides," he added, tilting his head in the direction of the bar, "you already got a first rate man. Roscoe Van Dyke over there has a pretty good reputation, leastways where I come from. You could do a lot worse than him." They seemed surprised by the endorsement. "And always keep in mind somethin' my daddy told me: don't trust a man who looks good, trust a man you *know* is good."

Thanks to the cowboys, parched from the trail, the drinks were flowing fast and furious. Pete, though a good hand behind the bar, was hard-pressed to keep up. He was taking some heat but held his tongue, all too aware that his customers were men who'd gotten through life with little learning, few social graces and a healthy thirst for anything that helped them forget their mean circumstances.

But alcohol had other, less pleasant side effects. It

made some men vicious and stupid and turned cowards into merciless killers. The combination of an excess of liquor and an intemperate personality could lead to unforeseen and tragic results. People became unpredictable, belligerent, eager for a quarrel. You never knew when trouble might break out...

It started when Waring was in the midst of another episode from his illustrious past, this one involving a fourteen-foot river crocodile that capsized his boat and pulled a native guide under, turning the water scarlet with his life's blood.

One hombre, well into his cups, took exception to what he considered to be a tall tale that strained credulity past the breaking point. "Mister, yer talkin' into yer hat. I ain't never heard anythin' so foolish in my en-tire life. Giant lizard! These others may put up with yer jawin', but I know a first class liar when I see one and I'm lookin' at one right now!"

Waring's reaction was not that of an infirm man. He sprang at the hapless cowboy, the two of them crashing to the floor. In a flash, Waring was astride his opponent, slamming his fists into whatever part of his anatomy the cowboy left exposed. And all the while he was howling epithets and abuse, his rage ungovernable. Seaver recollected that the victim of the unwarranted assault hadn't come in alone and, sure enough, another hard case was shouldering his way through the onlookers. Seizing Waring from behind, he dragged him off and hurled him toward the bar. Once he checked the condition of his battered friend, saw the extent of his injuries, he started toward Waring, but strong hands restrained him, many present shouting "He's blind!" and other sentiments to that effect.

Philip Waring was beside himself with fury. He'd landed in a heap beside the bar, slopping the contents of a spittoon all over everything in the vicinity, including himself. Lurching to his feet, he started throwing punches, flailing at anyone within reach. The others fell away from him, avoiding his windmilling fists. Seaver moved closer and Waring sensed his presence, whirling and letting fly with a vicious haymaker, which Seaver deftly slipped. Waring, off balance, was an easy target. Seaver stepped inside, delivering a short, brutal punch that landed exactly right. Waring dropped his hands, swayed and toppled to the floor like a felled oak.

The force of the blow jarred Seaver's knuckles. He walked away, kneading his sore hand, while others saw to Waring, pronouncing the damage slight. There was no shortage of volunteers to help carry the prostrate hunter back to his quarters. In the end, it was the mountain man and Roosevelt who claimed the honor.

Roosevelt sought to console Seaver as they bore their burden upstairs: "You were quite right acting as you did. Alcohol can have a deleterious effect on a man's reasoning. Still," he added, grinning, "I admire the chap's fire, don't you?"

Patricia opened the door and as soon as she saw her husband, her hand flew to her mouth. "He's fine, ma'am," Seaver assured her, "just a little worse for wear is all." She didn't seem inclined to take his word for it, checking her husband's condition once they'd shifted him on to the bed. As soon as she caught a whiff of him her expression changed. Straightening, her face set, she thanked them formally for their consideration and politely ushered them from the room.

"An excellent woman," Roosevelt observed as they made their way to the staircase. "Clearly upset by her husband's condition but discrete enough to hide it. Bully for her."

When they reached the main floor, the bearded man paused. "Po Cartwright," he informed them. "Be seein' you around." With that, he nodded and returned to the bar.

"That's Waring's man." Roosevelt said. "Reputedly the best guide in the area, blast the fellow. I would've retained him myself had Waring not gotten to him first."

Seaver commiserated with him, then started for the front door. "Think I'll call it a night."

"Yes, perhaps that's for the best." Clearing his throat. "If you don't mind, I'll walk with you a ways. I want to check our animals, see that they've been properly provisioned and bedded down."

"Plan on heading out soon?"

Roosevelt glanced at Seaver, a merry expression in his eyes. "Perhaps..."

They proceeded in silence, enjoying the cool air and good company. Roosevelt spoke first. "A singular man, Waring."

"I'll go along with that."

"What a life he's led! I've done my share of traveling and hunting, but Philip Waring is undoubtedly the greatest sportsman of our time." Seaver grunted in acknowledgment. "Visiting exotic climes and stalking the most fearsome animals. Placing himself in harm's way, living off his wits..." He sounded distinctly wistful.

"Still. A man likes to plant his feet somewhere. Have a little spot to call his own."

"True. My little spot is over in the Dakota Territory. Ever been there?"

"Can't say I have. But ain't you from back East originally? That accent of yours sure don't come from Dakota."

Roosevelt brayed with laughter. "You are a bold one, Mr. Thornton."

"Call me Frank."

"So be it. Frank it is. And, yes, I am a Yankee through and through, though I hope you will forgive that lapse in character on my part. I've tried but I simply can't escape my humble station." He clapped Seaver on the shoulder. "You're a good sort, Frank. A fine fellow. Just the type Waring needs on his Yellowstone safari."

"That may be. Truthfully, I haven't decided if I'm going along."

"Oh?" They stopped outside a corral. The barn and stables were barely distinguishable in the growing dark. The enclosure smelled of live animals, fetid and base. "He made it sound like—well, no matter. That is, of course, entirely your own affair."

"I hear you've got your own hunting party."

"How the birds do chatter. Yes, I've assembled a small company, stout fellows all. We'll be leaving for Yellowstone...in due course."

"I wish you luck. Your men are fortunate to have such a capable leader."

"Your confidence in me is most gratifying. But...returning to the subject of Waring." Roosevelt hesitated. "I shall rely upon your discretion."

"You have it."

"If you *are* inclined to join him—and my intuition tells me that's the case—you should keep one thing in mind." Theodore Roosevelt propped one boot on the bottom rail of the fence, assuming a comfortable position. "I'm a man who has some experience with tragedy, as you might have heard. I came west, in part, to leave all that behind. Perhaps for that reason I feel a special kinship with Waring, the pain that man must be enduring. His entire life turned topsy-turvy, his future uncertain and bleak." He scraped the bottom of his boot on the rail, spoke into the surrounding darkness. "Until I met Philip Waring I had not encountered a man who wished to die more than I do." His words lingered in the air around them, refusing to go away. "I trust I've made myself clear, Frank." Roosevelt shifted, facing toward him.

"Yeah...yeah, you have."

"Strange. I feel a certain kinship with *you* as well. You're older and our backgrounds couldn't possibly be more different. That said, I think it safe to say we both have some acquaintance with grief and loss. Am I not correct in that assertion? The more years pass, the more the casualties accumulate. It becomes an intolerable burden to bear. The sheer energy that is sometimes required to continue drawing breath while our loved ones perish around us. And so some of us knowingly court danger, push ourselves to the extreme limits of endurance. Less discerning souls think us fearless but there's more to it than that. We seek the precipice, risk life and limb *because we have nothing to lose*. The joy of existence is gone and those daring deeds of ours amount to nothing more than an expression of our desire to be put out of our misery. We're like wounded animals, Frank, awaiting the *coup de grace*."

As he made his way back to Essie's, Seaver reflected on Roosevelt's words and applied them to what he knew about Philip Waring.

A blind man in pursuit of a beast that had already killed and, even more worrying, showed no fear of encroaching humans. Was that not a death wish?

And where did that leave Patricia Waring? He could no

longer fool himself into thinking that his interest in the Warings was impersonal, above reproach. She was the most alluring and desirable woman he'd ever met and there wasn't any sense denying she was a major contributing factor in his decision to join the expedition.

He might not be able to save her husband from the inner demons besetting him, but he was determined to do his utmost for the hunter's lovely, young wife.

When he woke the following morning, he dressed and went out to Essie's light-filled kitchen to discover what the old gal had cooked up for breakfast. He feared he was becoming addicted to her hearty, delicious meals and his midsection was starting to show it. But upon entering the kitchen, he was surprised to find Roscoe Van Dyke already seated at the table, a napkin snugged in his shirtfront like a bib.

"You might be the luckiest man in Livingston," Essie informed him, nodding in Van Dyke's direction. "This overgrown galoot was about to eat both your breakfasts and ask for seconds."

"Now, Essie," the rotund lawman admonished her, "there's no call to be surly."

"Sit down, Mr. Thornton," she told Seaver. "Pour yourself some coffee while you're waiting."

The sheriff, it turned out, was far from a stupid man. He had correctly divined why Foley and Bauer had buttonholed him and was grateful for Seaver's words of support. Apparently they'd made a favorable impression on his employers.

At one point, after piling their plates high with pancakes and links of sausage, Essie left them to tend to other duties. It was then that Van Dyke finally got down to the real purpose of his visit.

"Mr. Thornton, I'm much obliged for what you did. And I'm not the kind of man who forgets when someone does me a good turn. Like, for instance," leaning forward, "if there was somethin' come down the wire about a certain fella wanted for killin' a deputy down St. Joe way. A notorious man, it turns out, and we're s'posed to use all due caution. There's even a circular although, to be honest, the likeness is purty poor." He paused to devour a sausage wrapped in a flapjack. "*Mmm.* This shore is a fine breakfast, innit?" He had to sit well back from the table to compensate for his girth. His napkin was spotted with syrup and dribbles of coffee. Favoring Seaver with a wry grin. "You got no idea how lucky you are, havin' that fine woman for a friend. I wouldn't do *nothin'* to cause trouble under her roof, you get my drift?" Seaver made no reply. Stared at him, not giving an inch. Van Dyke's bravado faltered. "I already told you, you got nothin' to fear from me."

"I already knew that." Seaver's voice was low, neutral. No explicit threat but the room had definitely taken on a chilly aspect.

Van Dyke looked uneasy. "Now, see here, Sea—uh, Mr. Thornton. When I said I wasn't fixin' on causin' you trouble, I meant it. There ain't no cause to be givin' me the snake eye."

Seaver thought about it, decided the fat man had a point. "I suppose you're right."

"Sure I am." Van Dyke looked relieved. "And I already told you, I wouldn't do anythin' to get ol' Essie mad at me. You done me a favor, now I done one for you."

"So we're even, is that what you're saying?"

"Naw." Van Dyke used the end of his napkin to dab his greasy chin. "How can we be even? We ain't never met, remember?"

◆ ◆ ◆

Later that day, Seaver stopped by the Albemarle Hotel and formally accepted Philip Waring's offer. He would join the expedition, asking no remuneration, only his share of victuals and upkeep. Waring was confused and a bit put out but quickly agreed to his terms.

Patricia Waring stood off to the side, trying not to show her relief.

In a few minutes it was over and he was back outside, striding down the wooden sidewalk, moving away from the Albemarle and toward a future he could neither control nor predict.

Well, Seaver thought to himself, *you've thrown in your lot with these people, now you're just going to have to wait and see what happens next.*

Trying to put the best possible face on his decision, even as part of him knew it was bound to come out badly in the end.

CHAPTER SEVEN

THE SUN HAD NOT yet fully risen as the Waring party assembled at Stein's Livery. The entire company would be present for the first time and Seaver made the most of the opportunity, observing and appraising each of his travel companions, identifying strengths and weaknesses.

Their intrepid leader looked a trifle peaked, likely nursing a splendid hangover. The amount of liquor Philip Waring consumed was worrying. Alcohol rendered a man untrustworthy, erratic. Better men than Waring had been bested by the bottle. Patricia seemed drawn and anxious, shooting nervous glances at her husband during a heated exchange with Kurt Stein over the final bill.

"An outrageous amount! You'd think you've been stabling an entire regiment."

"You're forgetting about the nigger and that bunch." Stein jutted a dirty thumb at Po Cartwright and his entourage. "They slept here every night and my lady wife was kind enough to bring them grub. You should be thanking me, Mr. Waring. Not many around here would put up with the likes o' them."

Seaver checked but Cartwright didn't react visibly to the remarks, though he must have heard them. He was a throwback to another time, solid as a slab, barrel-chested, immense across the shoulders, his heavy body swathed in faded buckskin, worn like a second skin. At least fifty years old but giving the impression of enormous strength and hard-won guile. It was said that Cartwright was acquainted with every rock and tree in Yellowstone and that even the Indians deferred to his knowledge of that wild, untamed land. He was conversant in a variety of tongues and had wintered with both the Crow and Sioux on a number of occasions. The latter called him "He-Who-Leaves-the-Tracks-of-a-Bear" and both tribes respected him enough to forgive him for fraternizing with their traditional foes.

Little Queen, his Indian wife, bore a fearsome reputation. Originally a Blackfeet, she had been captured by the Crow during a successful raid. But she proved so ornery in disposition none of the braves who tried to claim her as a wife had much success taming her. A number bore permanent scars for their trouble. A particularly ardent suitor was found groaning, badly concussed, on the ground outside his tepee. Rejected and summarily evicted. When she expressed a passing interest in Po Cartwright, the Crow chief leaped at the chance to rid his lodge of a difficult, vexing presence.

She was tiny, imperious, fierce. She'd nudge Cartwright to get his attention and constantly chattered at him, her vocabulary a mish-mash of three different languages, including pidgin English.

Still grumbling, Waring settled their bill, then, with mercurial swiftness, changed tack and started barking out orders, relying on his wife to see that his instructions were carried out to the letter. Seaver lent a hand loading the provisions onto the various pack animals Waring had either purchased or rented for the duration of their journey. Each of the beasts could bear loads of two hundred and fifty pounds. Besides food, there were tents, rifles, ammunition, cooking utensils, extra clothing, everything necessary for surviving ten days in the Hell-Roaring Creek area. Not a locale noted for its creature comforts.

He and Caliban frequently passed each other as they went about their duties, Seaver watching in amazement as he hefted sacks and lugged gear with his one good arm that most men would have trouble managing with *two* healthy, intact limbs.

At one point, Seaver paused, taking in his surroundings. "A good day wasted on hard work," he observed but Caliban only grunted. Still sulking about having to accompanying Cartwright and his kin to Cinnabar. But there were too many pack animals and someone had to tag along to help.

The youngest member of their company watched proceedings from a position beside her mother. Fawn was eight or nine years old and shy around strangers. She peered about, trying to follow what was happening, jumping when Little Queen laid a reassuring hand on her small, dark head.

"She's a great help to her mother." Seaver turned and found Cartwright standing nearby. The big man smelled ripe enough to chase off a skunk and Seaver had to resist an impulse to back up a step, allowing himself breathing room. "Quick as a fox too. She can catch a rabbit, skin it and cook it while we're still settin' up camp. You jes' watch her." They had been formally introduced earlier, both letting on they hadn't met previously. "The boss man speaks well of you."

"Is that what we're supposed to call him?"

"Boss man, *jefe, capitan*, it's all the same to me. As long as he crosses my palm with silver, I'll call him the King of Spain if he wants." They grinned at each other.

"What do you think of this deal?" Seaver decided not to mince words. "What are we getting ourselves into?"

"A blind man going after a mountain lion, that what you mean?" Cartwright spat an impressive distance. "Pure craziness."

"But as long as he crosses your palm with silver..."

"Ain't it the truth." Cartwright shook his shaggy head. "I am a damn fool for money. But did I hear right? You're doin' this for *nothin'*?" The guide was baffled at the notion. "Now that's plumb peculiar."

"I guess when it comes down to it, we're all damn fools."

"Well, then, let's jes' hope and pray one of us damn fools can keep *that* damn fool from getting his damn fool self killed." They watched Waring, scowling beside his wife. "So you're goin' on the train with 'em, are you?"

Seaver shrugged. "It seemed like the thing to do. Saves wear on my backside. Careful with my Nag, he's got a mean streak."

"That's what I hear. Why not take a different one?"

"Have you seen him?"

Cartwright nodded. "The big red bugger? A fine horse, no question." Casting a malicious glance Caliban's way. "Mebbe I'll add him to the nigger's string..."

"Just get him there in one piece. He'll beat anything those mountains throw at me."

"Ain't so bad where we're goin'. More like high plains. You'll see." They watched Caliban securing the last of their baggage. "Looks like that's that. Have a good trip. We'll see you down in Cinnabar."

"Couldn't he have gotten this stuff there or in Gardiner? Save you the trouble of packing it all that way?"

Cartwright smirked. "Man may be blind but he ain't stupid. Closer you get to the park, the more those outfits charge. Cinnabar ain't much more than a depot and Gardiner...well." He spat. "He wouldn't want his pretty wife exposed to *that* den of iniquity. Ain't nothin' there but saloons, gamblin' dens and whores." Caliban stalked past, surly, insolent, acknowledging neither of them. "*Huh.* Gonna be fun gettin' on with that one. Sour as an old maid and twice as ugly. Be seeing you, Thornton…"

For some reason, Waring felt compelled to make a short speech before the group departed. Seaver paid little attention, finding the whole thing ludicrous. While Waring went on about "the historic dimensions of this endeavor", Seaver gazed at Patricia. Like him, she seemed inattentive, her mind elsewhere. At one point their eyes met and he thought he saw her face color. After that, she didn't look his way again.

Before long, the advance party was underway. Cartwright, on his long-legged bay, led off the procession, a line of horses strung behind him. Caliban, Little Queen and Fawn followed with their pack animals, creating a ragtag caravan. They would make the journey over two days, overnighting with an outfitter friend of Cartwright's who lived near Emigrant before continuing on to Cinnabar the following day.

They moved through town, then bore southwest, toward Paradise Valley. There had been little rain for the past month so the roadway was solid, hard-packed, and they made good time. Before long, the mountains veered up before them, the loftiest peaks already fringed with snow.

Cartwright steered them through the narrow valley corridor, following the course of the Yellowstone River. Above the fast-flowing water, along a thin channel carved by powerful, primordial forces, the small, diverse party made their way, while the day grew brighter around them and Paradise did its best to live up to its name.

The next morning, Seaver packed his meager kit and prepared to take his leave of Essie Montgomery. He had every intention of making a quick exit, not stretching out his farewell. However, once he'd hauled his things to the front door he found himself reluctantly obeying a summons to join her in the parlor.

When he came in he found her waiting, arms crossed, her expression severe. "So," she began, "you've decided to join in this foolishness after all." He shrugged, ducking her eyes, practically shuffling his feet in embarrassment. Then she softened, tiring of the game. "Well, since you've already made up your mind I don't suppose there's any use wearing out my gums about it. And as a good, God-fearing woman, the least I can do is see to it you're properly armed." She stepped aside, revealing a long rifle that shone with polish and close attention. He could smell the gun oil from where he was standing. "Well, come and get it, don't just stand there, stiff as a post."

Seaver came over and stood by the weapon propped against the mantle. It was a .44 Henry, with a walnut stock, iron butt plate and rounded heel. Had to be thirty years old. A rare and beautiful thing. "Ma'am, I can't—"

"Of course you can. It was my Walter's and now it's yours."

He picked it up. It was a magnificent piece, a thrilling combination of form and function. Its barrel was two feet long, forged from the finest steel. He balanced it in his hands, finding its weight well distributed. The rifle, though heavy, was sturdy and dependable. It had a stalwart reputation and would have little difficulty bringing down a cat, a buffalo or anything else he might point it at. He turned to her, shaking his head. "This is too much, Essie. I know of few men who possess anything like it."

"It comes with a wood cleaning rod and I took the liberty of buying two boxes of cartridges. That should suffice."

He was well and truly flummoxed. "I...don't know what to say."

"Then say nothing," she replied, brushing past him, hurrying out of the room. "Just ride on out of here, Frank Seaver. And if you ever find yourself in this part of the country again—"

But she couldn't finish.

Que Dios se lo pague, Essie Montgomery.

May God bless you and reward your good heart.

Owing to mechanical problems, the train to Cinnabar was late getting underway. Despite the herculean efforts of its crew, the engine had trouble producing a full head of steam. The trip was made even *longer* by whistle stops at tiny communities and settlements along the way to drop off mail and cargo. The delays didn't bother Seaver. The arrangements in the day coach were, by his standards, luxurious. The seats were comfortable, upholstered in green plush. If required, there was a small stove to provide warmth for passengers and gaslights for when it got dark.

The layout was familiar. Except the last time he'd boarded a train he was masked, brandishing the Colt, helping a confederate relieve outraged passengers of their money and valuables.

The bad old days. He didn't miss them.

At one point, a freckle-faced youth entered the car, hawking newspapers and periodicals, sweets and the like. Did brisk business too, dispensing his wares and making change with an aptitude that impressed everyone present.

When he wasn't reading (Dickens again), Seaver gazed out the small, square window at the passing scenery or, more surreptitiously, spied on the wildlife *inside* the coach.

The Warings displayed little of the close, intimate contact one would expect from a married couple. Often, their only discourse consisted of him dictating long passages, which Patricia dutifully committed to paper and read back to him at his request. Presumably portions of his next book. Both were oblivious of the gorgeous country on every side, too immersed in their work to appreciate what they were missing.

The car's other occupants, tourists by the look of it, were more animated, moving from window to window, trying to get a better look at the passing terrain. Not a few of them foreigners, by the sound of it. Paying good money not to be bored. Rich people with funny accents and fancy duds, determined to enjoy the grandeur of America's Wonderland without forsaking the safety and comforts of home.

They reached Cinnabar late in the afternoon. Po Cartwright's depiction of the place as little more than a depot proved accurate. Except for the railroad station and a short row of wooden storefronts, there wasn't much to it. A low, weathered range formed a rocky backdrop, rising above the broad, barren plain. The location was level and featureless, the local flora consisting of sagebrush and prickly pear. But it was here the rail line ended; from this point on travelers had to find other means of reaching the park.

There was a flurry of activity once the train squealed and grated to a halt. Descending passengers were immediately hailed by agents of the various outfits vying to ferry them the rest of the way to Mammoth Springs and the new hotel where many of them had booked lodgings. Gradually they were shepherded aboard waiting coaches, Concords and "Tallyhos" boasting upper and lower seating, drawn by six-horse teams. The drivers manning these conveyances were merciless, aware of the gathering dusk, anxious to make good time. Furiously whipping their unfortunate chargers and cussing up a storm, they steered their swaying, top-heavy carriages out of the depot yard, thundering off toward Mammoth at the best possible speed. The new stage road through Gardiner Canyon would shave miles off the journey but it wasn't open yet, so they had to make do with the old Norris Road, a longer, more circuitous route.

The Warings and Seaver negotiated their way through the shouting tumult, bearing whatever personal baggage they'd brought with them. Exiting the train station, they found Po Cartwright, Caliban and the others waiting a short distance away.

The riders looked somewhat trailworn but otherwise in good shape. The pack animals had fared well and the trip from Livingston was virtually trouble free—at least according to Cartwright. Caliban's face told a different tale. The Nag had been up to its usual tricks, bedeviling him at every opportunity. After two days of its antics, he was mad enough to chew nails.

Despite the lateness of the hour, Waring was anxious to push on without cease. Roosevelt's party had slipped out of Livingston the previous day and Waring was convinced the plucky Easterner represented a serious challenge to the success of their venture.

Seaver didn't understand his reasoning. In such a vast territory, what were the chances of a transplanted Yankee stumbling across their cat? Having Cartwright along gave their group a distinct advantage. His knowledge of the country and habits of the creatures that made it their home was an invaluable asset. If anyone was going to find the cougar, the mountain man was the most likely candidate.

But Waring was insistent so they left the lights of Cinnabar behind them and traveled further along the road to Mammoth before darkness finally defeated them. They ended up bedding down in a shallow wash just off the track. Too dark to gather wood for a fire; after a long, taxing day of travel, most of them only interested in crawling into their bedrolls and closing their eyes to the world.

"Are we inside the park yet?" Seaver asked, once he was comfortably ensconced in his soogan. Cartwright and his Indian family also slept out in the open, disdaining the Sibley tent Waring offered, one huge buffalo robe encompassing them all.

"I reckon so," Cartwright confirmed, yawning. "Welcome to Yellowstone, folks."

"I didn't notice any signs."

"They keep talkin' about it but so far that's all it is, *talk*. Ah, damn," he groaned, trying to find a comfortable position. "I swear I'm getting old. Lookit me: sore 'n stiff as a board and still livin' like an Injun. What happened to the common sense God gave me?" Little Queen, snuggled into his back, murmured something and cackled. "You got that right, old girl. Not even *half* the man I used to be." Sighing. "Don't give a fella much to look forward to, does it?"

The next day found their spirits much improved. The morning was sunny, the chill soon lifting from the land. They breakfasted quickly and broke camp.

The roadway was dusty but navigable, wide enough for them to ride two abreast. On either side reclined scrub-lined hills, cedar trees and sage brush everywhere in evidence. The grade was increasing, becoming steeper with each curve and bend in the road. Those heavy coaches must have a hard go of it, Seaver thought. Pity the horses...

"Lucky it ain't been rainin'," Po Cartwright offered at one point, "this road turns into a quagmire right quick."

Patricia Waring laughed. "Don't sound so gloomy, Mr. Cartwright. Look around you! Give thanks for the bounty God has laid upon your table."

Seaver nodded agreement. Wise words. Since the beginning of the trip she'd risen even further in his esteem. As soon as they passed Gardiner, she had changed into a riding dress, her long skirt now sporting Turkish trousers, gathered in frills around lace-up, kidskin boots. She'd elected to use a standard saddle—a wise decision. A sidesaddle, while suitable for Sunday jaunts, would have been impractical over the long distances and rough country they would be traversing. She turned out to be a first rate horsewoman, certainly the equal of her husband. At ease in the saddle, prudent and firm with her mount, a black stallion of superior lineage, Arabian, by the looks of it, small-boned but strong, like most of its breed.

Waring's handicap had no perceptible effect on his equestrian skills. His horse was extremely well-trained, stepping carefully, smartly, sure-footed, with a smooth, gliding stride. Waring was enjoying himself, seemingly in his element. He didn't complain about the dust or the rising heat of the day and was content to let Cartwright lead the way. For now.

The breeze picked up at one point, gusting and swirling around them. After his battered hat was snatched from his head and cast into the roadway for the second time, Cartwright retrieved it, stuck it between his fanny and saddle. "Better," he grunted and continued on.

The wind soon blew itself out and Cartwright told them they weren't far from Mammoth Hot Springs. It should be coming up over the next set of hills...

They had only proceeded a short way when Po Cartwright abruptly raised his right hand, signaling them to halt.

Three Indian braves, mounted and armed, were fanned out, blocking the road. Their behavior was neither threatening nor benevolent, faces streaked and impassive. They offered no greeting, no indication of their intentions. Merely waited.

"Been expecting this," Cartwright muttered, spurring his bay forward to meet them. Seaver decided to accompany him, the .44 Remington reassuringly heavy on his hip. *As long as there are only three of them...*

Cartwright seemed to know the Indians, approaching the trio with no hesitation, calling out friendly greetings.

These were not the whipped, pacified savages the Great Father in Washington envisioned. They seemed taller than average, upright and confident. Traveling light, stripped down, the simplest equipment and tack. Very little in the way of provisions, relying on their skills and cunning to provide for them. Hunters and warriors, nomadic and far-ranging.

Seaver guessed they were Crow. Their outfits were varied, though they all wore leggings, waistcloths and beaded moccasins. One sported a tall, felt tophat, the others were bare-headed, black and white feathers jutting from long, carefully tended braids.

Two of them had Winchesters cradled across their thighs, the third a venerable Springfield.

One individual was clearly the leader. He offered a dignified, aloof mien that bordered on haughtiness. If there was trouble, he was the one to deal with first. He spoke at length to Cartwright, using his hands for emphasis. At various points he seemed to be scolding the guide but Cartwright took it all in stride. Once he'd said his piece, Cartwright responded, often in sign language, his fluency impressive. As he concluded his remarks, he gestured back toward the Waring party, jabbing two fingers at his eyes to illustrate his point.

The Indians regarded him with disbelief, glanced at each other, then burst into laughter. Clearly reacting to whatever information he had just imparted. In the midst of the merriment, their leader looked over at Frank Seaver, the brazenness of his gaze unnerving. His eyes still locked on Seaver, he said something to Cartwright and for the first time the mountain man didn't immediately respond.

He shifted in his saddle, addressed Seaver. "Pony-that-Walks wants to know why I have Death riding with me." Seaver refused to break eye contact with the Indian. They continued to stare each other down. The Indian spoke again, Cartwright providing the translation. "He says that Death makes for a poor traveling companion." Speaking out of the corner of his mouth, solely for Seaver's benefit. "Careful how you play this, Thornton."

"Tell him," Seaver instructed him, "I only bring death to my enemies." The Indian was nodding, not requiring a translation. Clever bastard knew more than he was letting on.

In halting English, he addressed Seaver: "Death an enemy to every man. Friend only himself." He directed a few more parting words to Cartwright, then the three of them wheeled their horses about, ascended a short hill and, in single file, entered a grove of aspen and pine and were soon lost from sight.

Cartwright was pleased to see the last of them. "Those were tough hombres. Some of Spotted Horse's boys, I reckon." Grinning at Seaver. "My friend Pony sure had you figured, didn't he?" Seaver glanced at him but didn't respond.

Cartwright briefed Waring and the others about the encounter, suggesting there was little likelihood they'd be further troubled by the local Indian population, news that was greeted with obvious relief.

"So they no longer think the cat is sacred?" Waring queried.

"Oh, I dunno about that," Cartwright hedged. "Let's just say I convinced 'em we ain't any kind o' threat."

Waring appeared puzzled but just then his wife spoke up.

"Do they have a village nearby?"

Cartwright scowled. "No, ma'am, not likely. See, this past spring the Crows were told they had pack up and leave the land of their ancestors and move to an Agency over in the Little Bighorns. Not far from where that ass Custer got himself kilt."

"For what purpose?"

"No food. Buffalo all gone, can't survive on fish. So this past April the United States Army escorted nine hundred people to their new home. Handed 'em hoes and seed, told 'em to give up their old ways and become farmers. Can you imagine? The greatest horse people the world's ever known, reduced to growin' turnips." Still furious, even months later. "They wanted to hire me to tag along but I told that Cap'n Armstrong, 'nossir, not for any price'." He went to spit, realized Patricia was present and suppressed the urge.

"But if the entire tribe was supposedly relocated," Waring wondered, "then who were those gentlemen we just met?"

"Some resisted, refused to go along. Spotted Horse is

their leader. Been hearin' lots about *him*. Faced down some railway surveyors awhile back, sure put the fear into them. Bound to be some killin' before all this is over and done with. Won't matter though. It's all been decided."

"What do you mean?"

Cartwright shrugged. "What is comes down to is they don't want Injuns anywhere near this precious park o' theirs. Don't want nothin' scarin' the tourists away. Tourists! *Pah!*" And this time he couldn't resist expectorating, considerately wiping his mouth with the back of his hand afterward. "They're ruinin' this country with their fancy lodges and guided tours. In a few years, this place will be overrun."

Patricia was looking about, trying to envision it and failing. "But it's so remote, won't that be a deterrent?"

"Let's hope so." Cartwright sighed. "Given the choice between tourists and Injuns, I know which ones *I'd* sooner have around. I don't wanna see Yellowstone spoiled, become a playground for rich white people and their brats. There are things I seen here you wouldn't believe 'less you seen 'em for yourself. The ground is alive, you can feel it rumblin' under your fcct in places. There's *power* here, power comin' right from the bowels of the earth. Wait 'til you see the waterfalls an' colored pools as purty as—"

"Yes, well, the important thing is you reassured those savages that we pose no threat." Waring was pleased. "Well done. Already you have proven to be a sound investment. Keep up the good work."

"Yessir." Cartwright saluted ironically and Waring heeled his horse, continuing up the winding track, Patricia and Caliban trotting after him. Once they were alone, Seaver caught his eye.

"You didn't tell him everything. Now let's hear the rest

of it."

"Shoot, Frank, I didn't know you spoke the lingo."

"I don't. What did you say to those Crows that they found so blamed funny?"

Cartwright smiled. "I jes' told 'em the truth. Informed 'em the man who hired me was as blind as the moon and had no more chance of hittin' that cat than I do of winnin' a rasslin' match with my Queen." Seaver had to laugh. "This whole thing ain't nothin' but a rich man's whimsy. The difference is, I'm gettin' paid for it and you ain't. Now if you'll 'scuse me, I'd better haul my fat ass up there and head off Waring. Maybe I'm superstitious but it don't seem right havin' a blind man leadin' the way."

CHAPTER EIGHT

THE VIEW FROM THE elevation overlooking Mammoth Springs was unlike anything Seaver had seen before. The hotel, four hundred feet long and built in the classic "Queen Anne" style, was the most prominent man-made feature, but the strange, unique locale in which it was placed reduced it almost to an afterthought.

The building was situated in a basin, ringed by steaming terraces that descended in discernible layers, each striated with different colors and patterns. Pipes leading down from these terraces fed hot water to the bathhouses. The water was rich with minerals and renowned for its therapeutic benefits. People paid good money to immerse themselves in tubs of it, especially after being assured, in no uncertain terms, that it was guaranteed to rid their bodies of rheumatism, gout or whatever happened to be ailing them.

"Ain't that something?" Po Cartright had edged up beside him. The Nag gave a warning snort to Fred, his bay, who promptly backed off a step or two.

"Quite the spread."

"Everything we see is due to volcanic activity," Patricia Waring explained. "The earth's crust is very thin here." Smiling self-consciously. "I've done some reading on it."

"As for myself, I'm looking forward to a hot bath and a soft bed to sleep in. Come, Patricia." With that, the Warings started down the steep hill, Caliban, not nearly as proficient on horseback, struggling to keep up.

"You stayin' at the hotel too?"

Seaver chuckled at the notion. "No, Po. Not my style. Just gonna find a spot to bed down and be ready to head out first thing in the mornin'."

Behind them, Little Queen, clearly impatient, spoke to Cartwright's broad back. "All right, woman," he retorted, "we're goin'. Hang on to yer britches. But, like I was sayin', Frank, if you want a cabin, a roof over your head, I know a guy. Jimmy Clark. A tough cob but a good man. There's always empty places, people off prospectin' or in jail. Jimmy'll find you somethin'. Up this high, September comin' on, you jes' never know. Weather's tricky. Might wake up with a faceful o' snow and *that* ain't too pleasant."

Seaver saw his point. "Maybe I'll take you up on that."

"You're smart staying away from the hotel," Cartwright said, just prior to moving off with his family, "I hear the place is goin' broke."

The problem was, the Mammoth Springs Hotel wasn't *finished*. Already two summers under construction and hammering and sawing could *still* be heard in various sections of the building. Many of the rooms were uninhabitable, progress slowed even further by a work stoppage (over unpaid wages) that had dragged on into July.

The rail spur from Livingston to Cinnabar was a godsend and eventually the tourists would come—not just five thousand, but ten thousand, perhaps even *fifty thousand,* and the hotel would flourish. Right now it was touch and go. Nowhere near capacity, under-capitalized, its creditors and shareholders clamoring for some kind of solution to the problem.

Morale was poor, the service terrible, the guests singularly unimpressed.

Seaver made one pass through the place, out of

curiosity, and detected an undercurrent of resentment and tension. He was loitering outside the restaurant when two old hens came out, one of them literally spluttering with rage.

"Did you hear what that darkie said to me? Why, if we were back home I'd have that boy hauled out and horse-whipped."

Apparently the poor morale trickled right down to the negro waiters.

He lingered awhile at a display in the lobby. A man named Haynes made a business out of selling copies of the photographs he'd taken of the park's various features. Seaver flipped through a catalogue while a clerk hovered nearby, ready to sell him the picture of his choice. Only to be disappointed in the end.

He eventually left the hotel and wandered about its grounds, no clear destination in mind. Every so often a wagon or someone on horseback would pass and he'd have to put up with the clouds of chalky, white dust they left in their wake. It was impossible to escape the stuff.

He went over to take a closer look at the "Liberty Cap", making a complete circuit of the upthrust cone before moving on to the steaming terraces. He scrupulously obeyed the posted warnings and kept to the prescribed path. Occasionally, the slope was quite steep, a hard slog, especially at that altitude. But the hike was well worth the effort; at various points he discovered standing pools of water stained in shades and tints he hadn't encountered before. He spent more than an hour, mostly alone, exploring the alien geology with boyish eagerness and curiosity. Feeling the heat of the ground beneath him, the warmth seeping right up through his boots...

A kind of tent city had sprung up around the hotel.

There were all kinds of wares and services for sale including, if he was not very mistaken, a discreet whorehouse. But what interested him most was the traffic in notions and curios. For a nominal fee, he could have a personal effect—say a spoon or button or comb—immersed for a day or two in a mineral spring, until it was permanently preserved in a coating not unlike alabaster.

Later that afternoon he came across Po Cartwright, the brawny guide showing the effects of a warm reunion with his old crony, the aforementioned Mr. Clark. "I gotta place for you to stay," Cartwright gushed, "c'mon, I'll show ya." He stumbled away and Seaver hustled after him. "All these people," he waved at the various enterprises they were passing, "ain't gonna be here much longer. The park is run by a symdicate—*syndicate* and they ain't gonna allow no private competition, know what I mean? They keep tryin' to put my buddy Jimmy outta business but he's too damn mean for 'em. But these other people—" He made a dismissive gesture.

They proceeded for some time before Seaver hazarded to ask: "You sure you know which—"

"Izzat one!" Cartwright waved at a stack of planks with a chimney. "This is Whiskey Charlie's place." He dragged open the door, nearly pulling the "cabin" down on top of him. They both recoiled from the accumulated aromas that came wafting out.

"This Charlie fella ain't part skunk by any chance, is he?"

"Naw," Cartwright gave Seaver a playful shove. "Somethin' crawled underneath 'n died is all. Let 'er air out a spell. You'll get used to it."

And after an hour or two, damned if he didn't.

◆ ◆ ◆

He woke early and hurriedly stoked up the stove. He'd unearthed the remains of some sort of dead, mummified animal in its belly, which accounted for some of the stink but not all of it. From the look of the place, its owner didn't put much stock in personal cleanliness. Seaver used his own bedding on the crude bunk and devoutly hoped it didn't end up infested with bedbugs or lice. Other than a fresh spider bite or two, he appeared to have escaped unscathed.

His joints and bones told him that though it might not have snowed overnight, the temperature had definitely dipped. Autumn in the mountains, with all the extremes of weather that entailed. A blizzard one day, sunny and mild the next. He mentally went through his gear, satisfying himself that he was prepared for whatever nature had to throw at him.

By seven a.m. he was ready to quit the cabin. Wandered over to the livery, checked the Nag, loitered about until the proprietor's sleepy son came down and he was able to settle his bill.

By nine, the Waring party, including a subdued looking Po Cartwright, prepared to set out on the next stage of their adventure. "We'll make for Yancey's but it'll depend on the roads. It's steep in places, hard on the animals, so we'll take it easy, 'specially if it's as hot as it's been." He was reluctant to say more. Seaver suspected it hurt to talk.

They headed east, the road fairly well maintained, they had been assured, for the first few miles, deteriorating after that. Yellowstone soon revealing its wild, untamed side, making no allowances for the comfort of travelers, insisting that part of the experience of Wonderland involve pain and inconvenience (and, occasionally, genuine peril).

It was a price more and more people seemed willing to pay.

◆ ◆ ◆

They stopped for lunch at a picturesque spot—where was Mr. Haynes now?—featuring a narrow, sluggish stream with a small island at its center. It resembled the setting of a fairy tale, Patricia observed, and no one demurred.

Once a light meal had been prepared and consumed, Seaver decided it was time to address a subject much on his mind.

"I've been hearin' a lot of tall talk and half-baked yarns about this cougar we're goin' after," he began. "Heard how many men it's supposedly killed and how fearsome dangerous it is. I'd sure like to know what the *real* story is."

They were in various positions of repose, the Warings and Caliban on one side of the makeshift firepit, Po Cartwright and his people on the other. The horses tethered a short distance away. Cartwright had advised against hobbling them. "They should have their legs free in case somethin' tries to get at 'em."

The atmosphere was relaxed, convivial. Fawn sat in her father's lap, dirty fingers twined in his beard, her head resting on his shoulder.

"Ain't had much experience with cougars, myself," Cartwright admitted. "Far as I know, most of 'em are loners and usually mind their own business." Pause. "Ain't no two cats the same, that's somethin' to keep in mind. Some of 'em are plenty smart. Like this one. Lots o' game in these parts but he's still kilt men. That's peculiar, you ask me."

"But wouldn't it regard us as just another form of prey?" Patricia wondered. "Not having much experience with our kind. Perhaps those who have fallen victim to it merely had the misfortune to happen across it when it was particularly hungry."

"Maybe one time, yeah, I might agree. But this thing's

kilt three people, mebbe more. I didn't know better, I'd say it *likes* the way we taste." Cartwright shot her an apologetic look. "'Scuse me for speakin' so bluntly, ma'am."

"But Mr. Seaver's initial statement requires a satisfactory response. Indeed, where *does* myth leave off and the truth, as it were, begin?" Waring lit one of his twenty-five cent cigars and expelled a lazy cloud of smoke that Fawn watched in rapt fascination. "I can tell you what I have gleaned from the various reports I've gathered. I've made every effort to separate fact from conjecture but, as I'm sure you realize, real, empirical evidence is rather difficult to come by." He shrugged.

"Let's hear it." Seaver dug out his Bull Durham and set about rolling a couple of cigarettes, one of which he intended offering to Po Cartwright, since Waring appeared inclined to be stingy with his fancy stogies.

Waring couldn't resist playing it up. He puffed reflectively, keeping them waiting, trying to build suspense. "Initial reports go back at least five years, is that not correct, Mr. Cartwright?" The grizzled scout nodded. "Since then the creature, unquestionably a superbly proportioned American mountain lion or *puma concolor*, has been sighted on perhaps ten or twelve occasions, sometimes only fleetingly. The single most lasting impression the creature leaves is its sheer *size*—on that point, the accounts are unanimous. Those who've had close brushes with it testify the animal is ferocious in aspect and seemingly unafraid of human beings. It has left ample evidence of its existence, including the carcasses of any number of deer and elk native to the area. Once again, the condition of the remains indicates a beast of considerable size. The bite radius confirms as much and someone supposedly recovered a tooth as big as a shot glass. In conclusion, I am convinced we are faced with a cunning, savage predator. It is very real, very large and considerably dangerous to any species that happens to wander into its vicinity. Including us."

"There's three dead men who'll testify to that. That is, if they was in any condition to do any talkin'." Cartwright reached across to accept a cigarette from Seaver.

Waring grimaced. "Various hunters, trappers and solitary travelers have ventured into the region and not returned. How many is not clear. This is a rough, treacherous country, ladies and gentlemen, and there are numerous fates that can befall the unwary and ill-prepared."

"So this cat may not be dangerous at all." Caliban spoke up for the first time. "Just doing what comes natural to it." No shrinking violet, this black man. A person unafraid to speak his mind.

"Ah, my friend, but it tasks us. It is ferocious and unafraid of our kind. That makes it all the more desirable to me. Think of the beasts we've hunted, you and I, often in places far removed from human habitation. Their one distinguishing feature is that they present an explicit threat of danger, the possibility that I might fail and pay the ultimate price for my folly. If we find and corner this beast, I believe it will prove worthy of its daunting reputation. If this is to be my last hunt, let's make it one for the ages. That's all I ask." He spoke with emotion and Patricia reached for his hand.

Cartwright poked Fawn, making her jump. "Well, I seen its tracks and I'll tell ya: it's like no cougar I come across before." He held up a big, slab-like hand. "Its prints weren't much smaller 'n this. How about that? Gave me the willies. Fresh too. When I saw *how* fresh, I hightailed it on out o' there. Ain't much puts the fear o' God into me, but grizzlies and big cats, they ain't too choosy about what they line their bellies with. Food is food."

"So you're sayin' that this critter has survived five years, likely longer, getting big and fat on anyone or anything dumb enough to cross paths with it." Seaver lit his smoke with a stick from the fire. "I'm with him," nodding at Caliban, "this cat's just doin' what its instincts are tellin' it to do. There ain't no blame in that, is there?"

Waring shook his head. "I believe you're both missing the point. It is a predator, a hunter. So are we. Our species are inimical. Both of us vying for a position at the top of the food chain. By virtue of our superior intelligence and industry, mankind *must* prevail or the natural order is defeated and we are reduced in status, undeserving of our inflated claims of achievement and progress."

Fine, high falluting words, Seaver thought. *But out here, beyond the pall of civilization, as arrogant and worthless as that twenty-five cent smoke.* "It's big and it's bad. Maybe a man-killer, maybe not. But *we're* the ones comin' after it, not the other way around." Seaver hesitated, then plunged ahead. "You're puttin' the rest of us in a tough spot. You want us to help you find it, track it to its lair and kill it before it kills you, maybe even one of us. That's a mighty tall order, especially for a man in your condition."

An uncomfortable silence ensued, everyone finding something to look at except the two principal players. But the liquor bottle hadn't been in evidence that day and that might explain Philip Waring's measured response.

"I know there are...questions relating to my personal health, some of you no doubt wondering, as Mr. Thornton does, whether I will be able to accomplish my stated goal. So be it. I suggest that a demonstration is in order. Caliban," he called, "you'll help me arrange things. We'll do it once we reach this fellow Yancey's establishment. It's time I put your misgivings to rest." He stood and his wife immediately did likewise. "Come, Patricia, let's walk awhile. It's certainly a lovely day for it..."

He gave the impression of leading the way but Seaver could tell she was the one doing the steering, directing him with subtle, almost imperceptible pressure. Otherwise, he might've ended up in the creek. Shortly thereafter, Po Cartwright produced a mouth organ and played surprisingly affecting renditions of "The Old Chisholm Trail" and "Dan Tucker".

As the notes of the last song faded away, Fawn was yawning, drowsy in the midday heat. Little Queen, meanwhile, was bustling about, packing up her cooking gear, ignoring the rest of them. One by one they rose and moved toward their horses. Reluctant to quit such an idyllic setting, practically dragging their feet to delay that inevitable moment when they would have to ride off and leave it behind.

About an hour later, they rounded a sharp turn and were brought up short. The road ahead was buried in boulders and loose debris. Part of an overhanging ledge had given way and now the trail was impassible. Two men, roughly attired and tight-lipped, unwilling to exchange more than token civilities, were sweating and cursing as they pried and leveraged rocks out of the way, creating a narrow passage.

Waring stayed where he was, but Seaver, Po Cartwright and Caliban stepped off their mounts to lend their assistance. Even Fawn hopped down to help. It was slow, grueling work but as the afternoon wore on they made headway and eventually achieved their goal, though the resulting channel was tight and serpentine.

With barely a nod of acknowledgement, the two men climbed aboard their animals and disappeared down the newly made path, moving with haste, perhaps even urgency.

"Poachers. Seen those boys around Cooke City. Hard cases." Cartwright spat after them. "Good riddance."

As Seaver was putting away his spade, he saw Waring take a surreptitious swig from a short, silver flask. *Bastard*, he thought, *here we are, breaking our backs, and he sits on his ass getting liquored up.*

"Mr. Cartwright."

"Yes, ma'am?"

Patricia walked her horse closer. "You indicated those two men were poachers. What is it they poach?"

"Anythin' they get their hands on, ma'am. Sell the meat, skins, whatever they can. *Their* kind is why we ain't got any buffalo any more. They'd as soon kill somethin' as look at it."

"Doesn't anyone try to stop them?"

"Well, it's a big park, ma'am. A lot of territory to cover."

"Treating a park like some sort of game preserve or animal sanctuary is absurd," Philip Waring snapped. "These are publically owned lands, belonging to the people of the United States of America." He was querulous, sitting slightly aslant on his saddle. Patricia regarded him suspiciously.

"I won't argue with you, Mr. Waring." Po Cartwright grasped his saddle horn, preparing to mount his bay. Then he spotted something and let go of the pommel. "But here's somebody who might..." He indicated the approaching rider, astride a fine-looking palomino. The newcomer was a dapper, well turned out dude, sitting stiffly in a brand new saddle. A silver badge caught the sun and Seaver heard Cartwright mutter: "Well, well...this oughta be innerestin'."

He brought his spotless, yellow horse to a halt a few

yards away. "Afternoon, folks. How are you doing?" Eastern accent. Another damn Yankee. There were more and more of them about these days. This one was about thirty years old, freshly shaved, moon-faced, eager. But his smile quickly faded once he took note of the unenthusiastic reception. Only Patricia's friendly greeting seemed genuine. "My name is Woodrow Dalgleish and I guess you can see from my badge that I'm an Assistant Superintendent here at Yellowstone. On behalf of Superintendent Patrick H. Conger and the rest of our—"

Philip Waring snorted in derision. "Save it, sonny."

Dalgleish looked startled. "*Wh*-what was that, sir?"

Waring, ignoring his wife's pleading glance, nudged his horse forward. "Last night I had supper at the hotel with some gentlemen from Bozeman. *Very* informative." Addressing his party. "D'you know what the locals call Mr. Dalgleish and his colleagues? Nine hundred dollar-a-year *rabbit catchers*." The assistant superintendent scowled, furious at the affront. His face turned the color of his stylishly knotted red neckerchief. "You have no power, no jurisdiction. You are a codpiece in a fifty dollar saddle." Po Cartwright sniggered.

Dalgleish struck back: "I'll have you know I am a duly appointed guardian of this park and I—"

"You, sir, are nothing more than a popinjay!" Waring roared. The poor kid almost toppled off his horse at the outburst. "If I could spare an hour or two I'd tell you *exactly* what I think about you and this Conger ass. His days are numbered and so are yours."

"Now—now, see here—"

"We have been greatly delayed, clearing this so-called road of yours and now we are very much pressed for time." Cartwright glanced at Seaver, rolling his eyes.

Dalgleish was flustered, anxious to win back control of the situation. "I, sir, am an employee of this park, appointed by the Secretary of the Interior. I am ordering you to—to respect my authority and—and—" In his frustration, he reached for his rifle. It was a foolish, petulant gesture. His hand only made it partway there before Seaver snatched out his .44, pointing it at Dalgleish's round face.

"You don't want to do that, friend." Seaver's voice was soft, low, *lethal*. Dalgleish paled, his hand frozen in position. "Go on, lower it." He did as he was instructed. "Smart lad."

"You idjit!" Cartwright snapped. "You coulda got yerself kilt, can't ya see that? You some kinda crazy man?"

"Yesser...I mean, nossir," Dalgleish agreed, all too aware that Seaver's pistol was still aimed directly between his eyes.

"You ain't no gun man, so don't act like one," Seaver told him. "Get yourself a sidearm, grow a beard, dirty yourself up some." Finally relenting and holstering his weapon. Caliban was chuckling but Waring had already lost interest. He'd gotten his horse turned around and was moving up the crooked path. Impatient to be on his way.

Seaver passed Patricia and saw that she disapproved of their rough treatment of Dalgleish. He could only shrug.

Po Cartwright caught up with him. "Heard you were pretty handy with an iron. Now I know they weren't foolin'."

Seaver wished he'd let it go. "He went for his rifle, I had no choice."

"That boy never stood a chance." Cartwright was looking at him strangely. Before he could say anything, defend himself, the mountain man was steering his horse away, letting him proceed alone. Clearly put out over something. People were hard to figure sometimes.

Patricia, meanwhile, was commiserating with the

assistant superintendent, who was still outraged at being so rudely handled. "I only wanted to find out your business. That's all." His voice rising: "What in blazes is *wrong* with you people?"

They stopped for the night in an alpine meadow near Blacktail Creek. Waring wanted to keep going but Cartwright over-ruled him. "Some hard travelin' ahead, boss. We don't want our horses all tuckered out. We'll make Yancey's tomorra and then head out from there. Plenty o' time."

There was ample forage and water nearby. Once they were encamped, there were several hours of daylight remaining. Cartwright went with his family exploring along the creek. Caliban was propped up against his saddle, his attitude one of self-reflection. Waring dozed in the shade of some nearby cottonwood trees. Seaver, noticing that Patricia was reading from a small, tan booklet, craned his neck, trying to see what it was. She finally looked up and showed him.

"It's Mr. Winser's guidebook on the park. I bought it at the hotel." She sighed. "I fear we're seeing but a tiny portion of the wonders this place holds."

"I'd like to see some of those geysers," Caliban said.

"For that, we'd have to strike *south* from Mammoth Springs, toward the Norris Geyser Basin."

"Too bad."

Seaver spoke up. "Maybe your husband will take you, once we're finished here."

"Perhaps..." But she appeared dubious. So did Caliban. The two exchanged glances and Patricia returned her attention to the guidebook.

After supper, Cartwright spoke briefly about the next

leg of their journey. "We'll cross a few bridges and once we leave the main road jes' stick close to me and mind the pack horses, see they don't get tangled up in the trees or bust loose. We don't wanna be chasin' 'em all the way to Saint Looey. Once we get to Yancey's, *huh*, that's when the fun *really* begins."

"Who's this Yancey fellow?" Philip Waring asked. "How did he manage to secure that location for his hotel?"

Cartwright's grin split his face in two. "Nobody knows. Somehow he convinced ol' Conger to let 'im set 'imself up in Pleasant Valley. Got a sweet deal goin' too. Does business with anybody in the neighborhood, no questions asked. He's a southerner, Kentuckian, I think. Still don't believe the South lost the war." He nodded at Caliban. "Your man should keep his distance. Ol' John, he might just—"

Caliban bristled. "I ain't his 'man'. I ain't *nobody's* man. You hear me?"

Cartwright was puzzled by his anger. "I hear ya."

"Then talk to me, not *him*." Pointing at Waring. "You think he's my owner or something? My *massa*?"

Cartwright shook his head in exasperation. "See what I mean? Boy, you get uppity like that around Uncle John, he's liable to lynch ya."

"Uppity, huh?" Caliban glared at him. "Believe me, you ain't *seen* uppity yet."

Cartwright seemed taken aback by the vehemence of Caliban's reaction. He turned to Waring. "We, uh, can get a few things at Yancey's, not much. Wet your whistle. Lay in a supply of fresh meat. Yer welcome to stay in his so-called hotel if you want but I wouldn't. He don't keep the cleanest inn, if you catch my meanin'."

"And from Yancey's...?"

"Across Baronett's Bridge and then northwest, where

we'll find yer cat. Hellroarin' Creek. Got some rivers to cross and there ain't no roads to speak of, not up there. No place for tenderfeet or soft arses." He spat into the fire.

"So we're getting close," Philip Waring mused.

"Yessir. Be there day after tomorra. Rain or shine. And so far we been lucky on that count. Least it ain't *snowed*."

"Only a matter of time," Seaver put in. "Seeing how cold it gets at night."

"I still don't understand why you people won't use the tents we brought along," Waring complained. "There's even a stove you can rig up."

"I got my buffalo robe. It got me through forty below, I reckon it can hack it here." Cartwright dug something out of his nose, flicked it away. "It gets bad enough, we'll take yer white man's tepee. 'Til then, I intend to lay back 'n enjoy the view."

CHAPTER NINE

THEY HAD JUST GOTTEN underway when Po Cartwright called out that some riders were approaching from the east.

"Can you identify them?" Philip Waring shielded his eyes against the slanting morning light.

Cartwright squinted. "Not Injuns. Horses, folks afoot. We'll jes' wait and let 'em come to us."

"Forewarned is forearmed, you mean."

Cartwright scratched his beard. "If you say so."

It turned out the party posed no threat to anyone. They were a family, five men and boys and two women. Sore of foot, careworn, almost played out. A broken axel had forced them to abandon their wagon and rig a crude *travois* between two of their horses, an improvised litter bearing their beloved patriarch. They hoped to make it to Mammoth before he succumbed from his injuries but Seaver didn't like their chances. At one time Josiah Trimble might have been a bull of a man, someone to be reckoned with, but in his present state he was much reduced, whimpering in pain, barely conscious. Privately, Seaver was of the opinion they'd be better off shooting the poor bastard and putting him out of his misery.

They were farmers, local people. Every year their family trekked into Yellowstone and spent a week or so camping and fishing. This summer they were determined to make a complete circuit of the park, allotting seven days for the endeavor.

They were at Sulphur Mountain, on the other side of

Mount Washburn, when disaster struck. The elder Trimble had been curious about a peculiar geological feature and ventured out onto a flat, crusty basin to investigate. Within a few steps his horse broke through the thin, brittle mantle, floundering into a bubbling, steaming pit, screaming piteously as it sank into the boiling cataract.

Trimble tried to leap free but lost his balance and slid in up to his waist. His sons got as close as they dared, managed to throw a line around him and drag him free. His legs and lower trunk were hideously burned, scalded to the bone by his immersion in the super-heated crevasse, which gave off a foul, noxious stench.

"Like the devil's own breath," was how the youngest son, Isaac, described it, shuddering and crossing himself. A weaker man would have died outright from shock but Josiah Trimble was made of sterner stuff. He'd spent the last two days in a delirium of agony and they still had a ways to go before there was any hope of relief. Each jolt or bump renewed his pain but his indomitable heart would not give out, his spirit stubbornly resisting death's soothing embrace.

"Lordy," Po Cartwright murmured to Seaver, "what's keepin' that man alive?"

"We can do nothing for you," Waring informed the Trimble clan. "Your father's condition is beyond our meager means." But Patricia insisted the family be given *something*, food, fresh, clean wraps to cover the festering, blistered flesh. She and Caliban did what they could and before long the Trimble family were on their way again, bound for Mammoth. It was a journey made in despondent hope, long hours spent in transit, compelled onward by their father's hideous injuries.

"What a way to die."

"I am afraid, Mr. Cartwright, that in my experience there are relatively few good ways to meet your end," Waring retorted. He nodded to his wife and she led him away.

"He's got her nearly as well-trained as that horse o' his, you notice that?" Seaver glared at him, offended by the comparison. "Take it easy, Frank, I didn't mean nothin'." Seaver watched as Patricia Waring disengaged from her husband and went to her stallion, which Fawn was holding for her. She exchanged a few words with the little girl and they hugged. The two of them had developed a rudimentary form of communication, Patricia picking up a few words of Indian lingo, though her pronunciation still frequently made Fawn giggle.

Even Little Queen was gradually warming to her, letting her help out with various minor tasks and duties. Fawn adored Patricia and that was a contributing factor. Whenever possible, two of them rode side by side, though the child's constant presence clearly annoyed Philip Waring. They passed Seaver and Cartwright, already engaged in an animated conversation, oblivious to everything except each other.

Women.

Suddenly he realized Cartwright was gazing at him, his expression canny. "Fine lookin' woman," Cartwright said, trying to sound offhand.

"You talkin' about your wife?"

The beefy guide guffawed, slapping him on the back hard enough to raise a bruise. "Frank, I swear. Sometimes you almost fool me into thinkin' you got a sense o' humor..."

"Uncle John" Yancey's establishment in Pleasant Valley was originally envisioned as a way station for the stage from

Cooke City. In the two years he had been at that location, Yancey had diversified his business interests and provided a number of services to a varied clientele.

The Waring party arrived saddle sore and sunburnt. In need of respite. But they took heed of Po Cartwright's warning and pitched camp in a field adjacent to the hotel, making it clear they were just passing through. To his credit, the proprietor didn't seem offended, sending out one of his men to invite them in for a drink and conversation. And, of course, they were welcome to replenish their supplies from his shelves or perhaps he could interest them in some fresh elk meat that had arrived, coincidentally enough, that very day...

It didn't take long for Waring to accept Yancey's offer of hospitality. He used the excuse that he wanted to survey the store's wares but Seaver was willing to bet the saloon was his first stop.

He stuck his head in later and wasn't impressed. It took up one small room and consisted of little more than a plank bar, puncheon floor and some homemade tables. Two wolfers looked up and narrowed their eyes at him. The lowest of the low. He let them be.

The "store" featured little more than the necessities, the shelves half full and badly picked through. Some canned fruit in dented tins caught his eye and an ancient container of *Lieby's Extract* but the price was too dear. He didn't much relish the notion of haggling with someone of Yancey's prickly disposition.

The owner/proprietor was bearded and hawk-eyed; there was definitely something of an Old Testament prophet to Uncle John. He despised Yankees and niggers and didn't think highly of Indians either. He seemed to be prospering without taking the slightest pleasure from his good fortune.

"The world ain't the same," he lamented to Seaver, "not since the war. Everything's changed. This ain't my country any more. And I got no place in it."

Philip Waring got things rolling immediately after supper. Interested parties were told to gather in a nearby clearing in fifteen minutes. No other information was forthcoming.

The others had no clue what he was up to. They followed Caliban as he carried a bulging canvas sack to the designated area, not far from their camp site. The contents of the sack grated and rattled as he set it on the ground.

"What d'you s'pose he's proposin' to do?" Po Cartwright was mystified.

Seaver yawned. "Man's got a point to make, I guess."

"Or jes' showin' off to his drinkin' buddies." Cartwright jerked a thumb toward Yancey and a number of bar patrons who had wandered over to watch, the wolfers among them. "Speak o' the devil: here he comes."

Waring, Patricia on his arm, walked toward them, shouldering an expensive-looking shotgun, its polished patina catching the golden light of the setting sun. Po Cartwright whistled. The weapon probably represented a year's earnings for someone like him. "Will you look at that..."

"I'm lookin'."

"Must be furren, British or German mebbe. A thing o' beauty."

Patricia appeared ill at ease, her mouth pressed into a tight, anxious line. Seaver felt something inside him shift as he observed her approach, so dainty and pretty. There was a vulnerability about her that made him want to go over and stand next to her, offer his shoulder for support.

Damn fool, he berated himself.

Waring joined Caliban and the mysterious sack. He faced the assembled company, clearly enjoying the attention he was receiving. "With the help of my associate, I will now demonstrate that while my eyesight might not be what it once was, it is still sufficient for our present mission." He nodded to the black man. "Proceed." Caliban reached into the sack and withdrew a white disk, five or six inches in diameter. "Mr. Yancey was good enough to sell me some odds and ends. I'm fond of shooting skeet and these bowls and saucers will serve that purpose nicely. Whenever you are ready, sir," he said, addressing his dark assistant.

He set himself, balancing on the balls of his feet, his posture alert, expectant. Seaver could hear the negro counting down and then with one fluid flick of his wrist, Caliban lobbed a saucer into the air. Waring's shotgun jerked up and he fired, the dish exploding overhead, falling to earth in splintered shards. Fawn squealed and clapped her hands vigorously, while Yancey and his bunch whistled and bellowed their approval. Waring soaked it up, playfully blowing on the muzzle, acting like it was nothing.

"Good shot, darling," Patricia Waring called.

"I'll be damned," Seaver breathed.

"They done this before," Cartwright speculated as Caliban extracted another saucer from the bag. "That darkie is in on it too." The next disk was dispatched with similar ease, the enthusiastic applause and cheers that greeted the feat egging Waring on.

"Notice he's using both barrels," Seaver pointed out, "he's trying to hide it as he reloads. Smart. Smart *and* vain. Dangerous combination."

Four saucers later, Waring missed for the first time. The hunter turned to Caliban and snarled something, a rebuke neither of them caught. But Cartwright's sharp eyes hadn't missed what had transpired. "The darkie changed his throw. Different angle. Lettin' us in on the trick, in case we hadn't already figgered it out fer ourselfs..."

The next five saucers never made it to the ground. Clear hits. Finally, Waring was satisfied that he had achieved his purpose. Lowering the shotgun, turning to them. "Well, ladies and gentlemen? Have I put your fears to rest?" Smug, thinking he'd pulled the wool over their eyes.

Cartwright spat, a slick, brown dribble streaking his beard. "Nice shootin'," he admitted. "You seemed to track them dishes all right."

"Mr. Thornton?"

He could feel Patricia's eyes on him but Waring's cockiness rubbed him the wrong way. "You're good with a shotgun," he allowed, "and when someone's settin' the table for you."

Waring's voice was tight with anger. "Your point being?"

"That expensive cannon's all right for target shootin'. But you won't be using a shotgun on that cougar and you'd better pray you don't miss."

"I *never* miss," Waring insisted.

But Caliban's mangled arm and livid scars cast considerable doubt on that assertion. Despite his boasts, Waring was *not* infallible. This demonstration had been for his benefit as much as theirs. He *needed* to believe in himself again. For the sake of his sanity, his marriage, maybe even his life.

His disability had robbed him of so much but he could not, *would not* permit it to take his pride as well.

That would be more than he could endure.

❖ ❖ ❖

They departed Yancey's early the next day. Philip Waring was nursing a dire hangover but determined to hasten their pace. The wolfers, who had been among his drinking companions the night before, informed him that they'd heard of a Yankee answering Roosevelt's description encamped on the south side of Coyote Creek. That was too close for comfort and Waring admonished Cartwright to do what he could to "make up for lost time".

"We ain't lost any time, Waring." Cartwright's mood in the morning was notoriously tetchy. "The animals are well-rested, we got fresh meat and a good night's sleep. I notice you picked yerself up a few bottles of Uncle John's finest for the road as well."

"So?" Waring eyes darted about but his wife wasn't within earshot.

"So now you need to realize some things. Where we're goin' is the *real* wilderness, boss, and we need everyone with his head screwed on straight. And that's all I'll say on the subject." He nodded to Seaver, who was standing nearby, and stalked off.

Cartwright ranged ahead of the rest of the party, scouting the terrain, leaving Seaver with little more to do than sit back and enjoy the view. Every so often casting glances toward Patricia Waring, who rode abreast her husband. Whenever he passed them, he'd touch his hat brim in acknowledgement and on one occasion received a smile and wave from her in return. A small thing, but he treasured it.

They paid the compulsory two-bits toll to Billy Jump, stationed on a hill on the east side of Baronett's Bridge. Billy was something of a character. He lived alone in a spartan cabin and passed the time by reading books. Dime novels, periodicals, old catalogs, anything he could lay his hands on.

Had no need for human company; owing to an accident of some kind he wasn't quite right in the head, although Seaver found him personable enough. After the others rode on, he paused at the bridge, admiring its workmanship, built under trying conditions, a dangerously fast river churning and frothing beneath it.

"I liked the old one better." Seaver turned and discovered Jump had joined him. A small, unassuming man, content with his place in the world.

"There was a different bridge here?"

Jump nodded, his expression woeful. "The Nez Perce burnt it down, mebbe seven years ago. Jes' a simple thing but it was *beautiful*. Hardly any nails or iron, jes' timbers."

"I guess this one does the job," Seaver offered, indicating the sturdy span.

"But now more people come through and more *traffic*," Billy Jump complained. "With their wagons and noise. Too many dang people..." He started up the path toward his tiny cabin. Raising his hand, a distracted wave. Muttering to himself. "Yessir. Sometimes the old ways is best. No need to change what's jes' plain good enough..."

Po Cartwright hadn't deceived them. The country approaching the conical, granite peak of Hellroaring Mountain may have been attractive to the eye but for mounted riders there were numerous ranges of hills to surmount, rivers to ford, acres of toppled deadfall to bypass and other hazards and obstacles to overcome before they achieved their destination.

The pack animals complicated matters and the weather didn't help either. It was another scorcher, so during the early afternoon they decided on an extended break to escape the worst of the heat.

They found a spot in a hollow, shaded by a copse of aspen and Douglas fir, close to a clear, frisky stream. Seaver took refuge under a tree rooted in the low, sloping bank, propping himself up against its gnarled trunk, a copy of *Great Expectations* on his knee. The book was well-thumbed, its spine cracked, some of the pages falling out if he didn't hold it exactly right. He was a slow, careful reader so he hadn't gotten far into it when something tugged at his attention. He glanced around, seeking the source of his unease.

He could see Cartwright dozing at the edge of the trees, Waring and Caliban huddled together near the horses. He closed the book and wandered over to where the guide was sprawled, nudging him with the toe of his boot. Cartwright started awake. "Huh? Wazzat?" Blinking up at Seaver. "What the hell, man? I was havin' a l'il shut-eye—"

"Where're the women?"

Cartwright scratched himself. "I dunno. Fawn wanted to pick mushrooms for supper. The Waring woman said she'd go with her..."

Seaver glared at him. He searched the immediate area but they were nowhere in sight. *Gone.* When he rejoined the others, Cartwright was talking to Little Queen, who had been cutting up some of Yancey's venison, her arms red to the elbows. He turned to Seaver, his expression sheepish. "She says the same thing. Out pickin' mushrooms."

Seaver wanted to clout him. "Did they take a gun?" Clearly, Cartwright had no idea. Cursing, Seaver ran to the Nag, yanked the Henry from its scabbard. Checked its load, while Cartwright hovered nearby. Waring and Caliban were gazing over at them, curious at the commotion.

"Queen says they went yonder," pointing, "likely only a little ways off. You're gettin' yourself all worked up over nothin', Thornton."

Seaver glared at him. "You'd better pray they come to no harm, old man. 'Cause you know at least *I'll* be coming back..."

Fawn led them further into the forest, taking advantage of a rare opportunity to work off some her boundless reserves of energy. She danced and capered around Patricia, tugging on her arm, the two of them largely incognizant of anything but the beauty of the day and their mutual affection.

Together, they scoured the ground for the white heads of mushrooms or other delicious tubers and roots. The child knew which ones were edible and which to discard, holding her nose when she came across a particularly toxic variety. The breadth of her botanical knowledge was astonishing for someone of her tender years.

At one point she skipped ahead and Patricia lost sight of her. "Fawn? Fawn? Where are you?" She heard a giggle from the other side of a thicket sporting a variety of red berries that Fawn had mimed were good for treating stomach ailments. "Don't run too far, dear."

"Come!" Fawn called. "Catch me..." Her voice already diminishing as she darted away.

"Here I come," she said, pursuing, the bag of mushrooms held tightly in one hand. Her skirt was a nuisance but the Turkish leggings helped, allowing her far more freedom of movement than women's apparel normally accommodated. The fashion conscious ladies at *Godey's* might not approve but they never had to ride a headstrong horse twenty-five miles a day, or go without basic necessities, existing under the most primitive conditions...

She discovered Fawn in a glade of waist high grass.

Insects buzzed and birds chirruped above them. The little girl waved merrily. Patricia was about to call her back, but at that moment a black bear cub popped its head up a few yards behind where Fawn was standing. When she heard its plaintive bleat, Fawn spun around, the girl and the cub equally astonished to be at such close quarters. For a few seconds, they merely regarded one another.

"Fawn," Patricia called, trying not to let her fear show, "Fawn, back away. Do you hear me? *Back away...*" Meanwhile, her eyes were scanning the area, knowing trouble wasn't far away.

But the child was intrigued by the cub, which was likely only a few months old, and seemed oblivious of her predicament. She crouched, holding out her hand, making clucking noises to reassure it.

The tactic backfired.

Instead of being pacified, the cub reacted with alarm, bawling and retreating from her touch.

From an adjoining thicket came an answering grunt and Patricia's heart raced as a sow backed out, alerted to the plight of her errant youngster. She was big and fairly old, showing numerous battle scars and worn patches on her dark coat. Her hackles rose as she detected an exotic scent. She growled a warning, her cub answering with a distressed keening sound...but Fawn was between it and her.

"Sweetheart," Patricia said, keeping her voice as calm and reassuring as possible, "you've got to get out of the way..." Her eyes darting about—*ah*! Inching over, kneeling, feeling for the broken tree branch, not wanting to take her eyes off the she bear. The branch was about four feet long and looked partially rotten. Not much of a cudgel but it was all she had. Summoning her courage. "Fawn, listen to me. You have to come to me and you have to do it right *now*.

Just back away, honey."

But the child was petrified, rooted to the spot. The female black bear was exhibiting threatening behavior, huffing and snapping her jaws. The cub broke the impasse, scurrying around Fawn and racing toward its mother. Fawn looked at Patricia, who gestured to her.

"*Come on!*" She started running, brandishing her makeshift weapon, resolved to defend Fawn even if it meant placing herself in mortal danger. The sow was tearing through the tall grass and it was unclear if she was collecting her offspring or attacking a perceived threat.

And then, lo and behold, Frank Thornton came running to the rescue, shouting and firing his rifle in the air. The racket terrified the bears, who scampered off into the surrounding trees, crashing through the undergrowth in their haste to escape.

Patricia dropped the branch and sank to her knees, sobbing in relief. Fawn ran up and threw herself down beside her, watching, abject and miserable, as Patricia wept. She touched her shoulder, repeating, in faltering English: "Fawn sorry, 'tricia, Fawn sorry..." Patricia rallied herself and Fawn, anxious to please, helped her to her feet. The two of them embraced, then turned to their benefactor, who looked on from a short distance away. Fawn approached him, reached out and squeezed his fingers. He smiled at her, gave her head an affectionate rub.

"Good to see you too, young lady." She giggled, ducking away from his hand.

Patricia was outwardly composed but her voice shook with emotion. "Frank, you are a godsend."

"Just good timing, ma'am, that's all." Brushing off his good deed. "Looked to me like you were fixin' to take on that big sow all by your lonesome."

"That's because I am a total and complete ninny," she said, hanging her head in shame. "I neglected to bring a gun. We were totally defenseless and it's my fault."

"Naw," he disagreed, "nine times out of ten, nothin' would've—"

"I'm glad you didn't kill her. She was only protecting her cub."

"I figured to scare her," Seaver acknowledged. "Could be that ol' gal knew a Henry when she heard one and decided to skedaddle." He rested the rifle across his forearm. "If you like, I'd be happy to accompany you on any future excursions, just to be on the safe side." He colored. "You and the kid, I mean."

"Maybe you could loan me your gun."

"It's got a kick to it."

"I'm an excellent shot. My husband taught me."

"If you say so."

"What's the matter?" She teased. "Don't think a woman like me can take care of herself? I need a man to protect me?" He looked down, smiling. "Why, Frank Thornton, I do believe you're blushing..."

CHAPTER TEN

PATRICIA WAS PROFUSE with her apologies when they returned to camp. The others had been alerted by the gunfire and were anxious and expectant. Patricia approached Little Queen and tried to explain, as best she could, what had happened but was summarily rebuffed. Instead of being appeased, she grabbed her daughter's arm and began to savagely berate her, Fawn absorbing the tongue-lashing stoically. The message was clear: *this stupid white woman might not have known any better but* you *should have.*

Seaver watched Patricia walk toward Waring and Caliban. Her husband took her hands in his, speaking earnestly to her. Caliban moved off, allowing them privacy.

"You sure can tell a Henry when you hear one," Po Cartwright said. "Mind if I have a look?" Seaver handed him the rifle and Cartwright put it through its paces, his admiration apparent. "This is some piece, Frank."

"It was a gift." Waring was approaching them, alone, both Patricia and Caliban hanging back.

"You don't say?" Cartwright sighted down the barrel. "Well, since yer a man who clearly knows his weaponry, I got something to show *you.*"

He passed the Henry to Waring and went off toward his gear. Waring expertly examined the rifle, tracing its lines with his fingers. "I've always liked the Henry," he confided. "Reliable, accurate, excellent craftsmanship. I have no doubt that it can dispatch any creature alive, save perhaps an African elephant." He held out his hand. "Frank, I want to thank you for taking such decisive action. You prevented a tragedy and possibly saved two lives today, including my wife's. I'm in your debt, sir."

Seaver shook on it but his eyes were on Patricia. And she was looking right back at him. Caliban stood off to the side, missing nothing, his expression enigmatic, impossible to decipher.

"Here ya go." Cartwright had returned with his prize, offering it for Seaver's inspection. "Ya know what this is, Frank?"

"A Hawken." Seaver was smiling. "Good Lord. Look at the length of that barrel."

"Thirty-eight inches," Cartwright informed them proudly. "See the mounts? That's iron, not brass. Maple stock. You could drop this off a cliff, drag it behind a mule team twenty miles an' it would *still* fire true."

"I've never held one." Seaver hefted the rifle. "Heavy brute."

"Eleven pounds."

"Accurate?"

"Up to two, three hundred yards."

Seaver caught his eye. "Let me guess. This genuine mountain man rifle was presented to you by none other than Jim Bridger or Joe Meek himself."

Cartwright chuckled. "Naw, won it in a game of 'Seven Up'."

"Now *that* I believe..."

It was a hard ride. At times, the slopes they were traversing were so steep, they had dismount and lead their horses to the top. Some of the pack animals balked at the maneuver, one of them losing its footing and taking a bad tumble, spilling their precious supplies down the rocky hillside. Fortunately the animal suffered no serious injuries, though the fall only served to make the brute even *more* disagreeable. They took turns pushing and pulling it to the top, giving it the occasional ill-tempered swat to speed its advance. After skirting some steep-sided granite buttes, the party descended into a long, narrow plain tucked between the surrounding ranges.

It was at that point, around four in the afternoon, that their guide announced they had officially entered cat country. "This is right near where I found them tracks I mentioned." He raised himself up in his stirrups, cast his eyes as far as he could see. "Good huntin' ground. Wouldn't have no trouble findin' plenty to eat."

"Then we shall make our base camp here," Waring decided. "As soon as possible I want you on the lookout for any fresh signs."

It was an ideal location. The Hellroaring River swept past on the left, eventually joining up with the Yellowstone, adding to its prodigious volume. There was ample pasturage, firewood, shelter (if they required it) in nearby groves of cottonwood, spruce and alder. Shrubs and bushes sported numerous types of edible berries, available for picking. Their stores were in fairly good shape but, even so, as Cartwright had observed, the area boasted a surfeit of wildlife, including an abundance of rabbits. Food would *not* be a problem.

It was magnificent country and Frank Seaver was absolutely smitten with it. The scenery on every side was captivating, and though Mr. Haynes' pictures conveyed some aspects of Yellowstone's natural beauty, he couldn't reproduce the experience of actually standing here, taking it all in. There was no other place like it on earth. Too many natural wonders to count. Even the air was different, its thinness intoxicating.

Mountains towered on every side but here, on this dry plateau, it was meadows and woods, prairie grasses and sagebrush, an environment unto itself. Even as he helped set up the camp, he'd find himself pausing in the midst of some chore and straightening, taking a long moment to survey his surroundings. He felt sympathy for Philip Waring, who couldn't bear witness to the ageless, unspoiled beauty of their mountain meadow, too blind even to see those same qualities present in his sweet-natured wife.

But there was something else, something that had been bothering him from the moment their party crested that last hill and discovered this lovely vale. He felt an immediate and inexplicable *familiarity* with the place, even though he'd never been within a thousand miles of here. There was a certain rocky promontory that jutted out into the river and a distinctive mountain peak that tweaked some distant memory—

Then it came to him: what he was seeing *exactly* duplicated some of the dreams he'd had during his ride from Missouri. Which was impossible, patently ridiculous. Such things defied logic and would only invite derision so, of course, he said nothing to the others, chalking the whole thing up to coincidence. Best put behind him.

Little Queen soon had them gathering fuel for her cooking fire, with the strict admonition to avoid cottonwood because it burned too quickly when it was dry and not at all if you so much as—as—

"Er," Po Cartwright amended, frowning at his sharp-tongued wife, "I think she means *spit* near it."

As soon as he could, Seaver snuck away on his own, finding a spot on a natural hummock and making himself comfortable. Rolled a thin cigarette, put a match to it.

Opened his book, settled in and commenced reading...

"Excuse me, Frank."

He'd been so deeply absorbed in *Great Expectations* he hadn't heard her approach. He used his thumb to save his place, rose to his feet, self-conscious and abashed.

"Ma'am?"

She, too, was hesitant, nervous. "I apologize for interrupting your reading. That's a particular favorite of mine as well. Dickens is such a wonderful storyteller, though at times I find his work disturbing. Especially when he describes the suffering of children."

He nodded. "I know what you mean. *David Copperfield* was like that for me. I read real slow and there were times in that book I wanted to race through parts, it brought me so low." He looked down at the battered volume. "Still. I guess that's the way life is too, when you think about it. You wanna get through the bad stuff quick as you can and hope for a happy ending."

She smiled. "That's very profound. Wise words. May I borrow it after you're done? I haven't read it for a number of years and I remember liking it very much."

"You can have it now, if you want." He held it out to her. "I've read it more times than I can count. I only got four or five books and good ones are hard to come by. So I gotta make do. Sorry it's in such rough shape..."

"I have quite an extensive collection," she said, brightening as something occurred to her. "Perhaps when we get back to Livingston we could do a swap. Do you like Mark Twain?"

"I was real fond of *Tom Sawyer*."

"I have that one and I also brought along *The Prince and the Pauper*. Do you appreciate poetry?"

The question flustered him. "Well, I suppose—"

"—because I have a volume of Whitman's poems, if you're interested. I admit, I find some of it quite baffling but you might like it."

He lowered his eyes. "Well, ma'am, I'm obliged but, like I said, I'm a mighty slow reader. I don't know how long it would take me to—"

"Oh, bosh!" She cried. "I'm happy knowing someone else is reading and appreciating fine literature."

"I thank you for your generosity." He hesitated. "Was that all, or...?"

It was her turn to blush and it looked much better on her. "Ah. Yes, ah..." Starting again: "You, ah, offered to accompany us on our next foraging expedition. If you'll recall, the last one was rudely interrupted."

He smiled. "I seem to recollect that."

"Well, Fawn says her mother needs more herbs for her cooking pot and since my husband is resting and both Cal and Mr. Cartwright seem to be otherwise preoccupied..." He saw the two men over by the horses. They were seated on the ground, each holding a fan of playing cards. Cribbage, by the look of it.

"Happy to ride shotgun for you."

"Fawn's mother is coming along this time."

"In that case, we're *guaranteed* to be safe."

"Oh, Frank..." Giggling. "Say what you like, she is an amazingly practical woman. Like a human whirlwind. Always turning her hand at something."

"It's how her people have survived, under the worst possible conditions. I got a whole lot of respect for Indians and how they live. So free and honest."

"I couldn't agree more."

"I'll just get some things," he said, starting back.

"It's certainly a beautiful day to be out and about."

It was indeed. *Especially if you happened to be escorting the lovely if unattainable Patricia Waring on a walk down some lonely forest path.*

The sun was arcing toward the western peaks and the wood in the firepit had nearly burned down to red-hot coals, just about perfect for cooking. They wouldn't have long. The heat of the day was much diminished and a gentle breeze stirred the surrounding grass, moving with visible effect through the trees ringing the camp. The air was fragrant with a variety of scents, some thick and cloying, others almost insubstantial, stray wisps that defied identification, rarely lingering, quickly dissipated.

As they were leaving, Seaver waved to the card players, letting them know the direction they were headed. They acknowledged his signal, then returned to their game.

Fawn and Little Queen roamed ahead of them, though he made sure they were always within sight. They scanned the ground with admirable concentration, occasionally whooping with pleasure when they spotted something particularly noteworthy, a mushroom or cluster of truffles. Patricia Waring seemed content to be out and about, enjoying her surroundings, tipping her head back at a sudden outburst of birdsong or collecting the occasional wild flower to add to her growing bouquet.

Seaver tried to give the impression of vigilance but, truthfully, most of the time he was watching *her*, her face, the pleasure she derived from her surroundings, a new spectacle greeting their eyes at every turn. Her joy was intoxicating, alluring, inspiring silly thoughts, elaborate and unconvincing fantasies that he could never sustain for long.

"It's certainly reassuring having you along," she said, startling him from his reverie. "You and your impressive gun. Sorry, the term is *rifle*, isn't it? My husband is constantly correcting me when I fail to make the distinction."

"Don't matter, they both do the same thing."

"You're very kind." They walked awhile, then: "So it's a famous rifle?"

"The Henry? Well, y'see Henrys around but not many like this one. I don't know much about art but this..." He took it from his shoulder, showed it to her, the beautiful veneer, each component perfectly tooled, painstakingly wrought. "This is like a painting or sculpture to me. A rare thing, perfect in every way."

She held out her hands and he gave it to her. She examined it closely, nodded. "It is certainly beautiful in its way." Glancing up at him. "But deadly too. Designed and manufactured with the intention of killing. The *Mona Lisa* isn't lethal: this is." Raising it, squinting down the barrel.

"The sight pops up..." He showed her.

"And you say it's accurate?"

He smiled. "Any...*gun* is only as accurate as the person holdin' it. The steadiness of their nerves, their willingness to pull the trigger." She lowered the Henry, returned it to him and they continued walking.

"My husband believes..." Taking a breath. "He thinks you're a *shootist*. I believe that's the term he used. That's partially why he wanted you along." Seeing his expression darken, she hurried to mollify him. "He wasn't passing judgment—"

"If you say so." His jaw was clenched, anger surging through him.

Her hands rose and fell. "I fear I've offended you. I should have remained silent."

"What your husband thinks," Frank Seaver said, his

voice low, almost a growl, "is of little concern to me. What *you* think, however," again they had stopped, "matters a great deal."

It might have been nothing, a trick of the light or his own desire clouding his perceptions, but he thought saw something flicker across her face. It passed in an instant but he registered inner turmoil, torn allegiances. "Frank," she whispered, reaching out but not *quite* touching his arm, "you...we must not speak like this. It achieves nothing."

"You're probably right." Not taking his eyes off her. "But at least it's out in the open now."

She bit her lip, glanced away. "I think we should be heading back, don't you?"

He put thumb and forefinger to his lips, whistled sharply. Fawn and the Little Queen halted and looked back. He gestured for them to return and they obeyed, retracing their steps, collection bags weighed down with various delicacies. They showed Seaver and Patricia their best finds, Little Queen pointing at various dirty clumps and going "Mmmmm" to make her point.

"I'd say we're in for quite a spread," he said, once they'd moved off. Fawn could restrain herself no longer, sprinting ahead, her mother pursuing her, making good time too, despite her stumpy stature.

"What a little vixen she is!" Patricia exclaimed. "Absolutely fearless."

"It's the age. It's only later you realize how fragile life really is." She looked up at him, an odd expression on her face, difficult to decipher.

He would have wagered five dollars, however, that he had surprised her yet again.

The mountain light was deceptive, so that by the time

they emerged from the trees, it was nearly dusk. As soon as they walked into view, all hell broke loose.

It turned out that Patricia had concealed the fact that her husband hadn't been resting, he had retreated to their tent with a bottle of Yancey's hooch. He polished off its potent contents and when he emerged, he was, by all accounts, in an ugly state of mind. He immediately inquired after his wife, Po Cartwright reluctantly informing him that she was off in the woods with Fawn, Little Queen and, oh, yes, Frank Thornton as well.

"The man near went crazy," Cartwright told Seaver later. "Started cussin' like a sailor 'til he was jes' about foamin' at the mouth. You couldn't talk sense to him. Even the nigger tried and you shoulda seen what *he* got for his trouble."

As soon as Waring heard his wife's voice, he bellowed and charged toward them. Confronting her, possessed by rage, he commenced *ranting* at her, vile epithets that shocked those present. At first Patricia cowered, then she pushed past him, running toward their tent, hands clapped over her ears, her little bouquet left scattered on the ground. Caliban stepped out of the way, watching as she disappeared inside. Then he planted himself directly in Waring's path, blocking further progress. Waring skidded to a stop and remonstrated with him, ordering him out of the way.

Caliban refused.

Philip Waring struck him, an open-handed swipe of considerable force. Caliban's lip was gashed, blood trickled down his chin. Still he refused to budge.

"That sonofabitch," Seaver barked, starting for Waring but, in turn, finding himself intercepted by Po Cartwright.

"This ain't none o' yer business, Frank."

"The hell it ain't."

158

Crack! Another slap raised a welt on Caliban's cheek. "Get out of my way, you black bastard," Waring snarled.

"No, sir, I will not."

"Po, let me at him," Seaver implored.

"*Wait*," Cartwright hissed.

Waring swung again, this time with a closed fist. Caliban caught it, held it gripped in the powerful fingers of his good hand, the one that hadn't been rendered useless in service to the man beating him. "No, sir, I won't move and no, sir, you will never, *ever* lay hands on me again." He was *squeezing* and Waring mewled in pain, gradually forced to his knees as Caliban applied more and more pressure.

"That's enough, Cal," Patricia Waring spoke from inside the tent. Not a command, closer to a *plea*. Nonetheless, he instantly obeyed and Waring slumped to the ground, cradling his hand, meek as a mouse.

"Y'see," Cartwright murmured, "all settled."

But it wasn't. Not by a long shot.

Seaver couldn't forgive the terrible things the man had said to his blameless wife, the slanders he'd offered her. The cowardice and weakness displayed by someone who should feel *honored* to be her husband and life partner. That couldn't go unpunished.

In the morning, once Waring sobered up, he'd give a demonstration of his own. And it was one he didn't think *any* of them would soon forget.

CHAPTER ELEVEN

SEAVER WAS THE FIRST to rise and Waring, owing to the delicate state of his head, the last to rouse himself.

It had been necessary to have an accomplice in his scheme and Caliban was only too willing to lend a hand. Clearly, he was still smarting from the incident of the previous evening and happy, eager even, to participate in the venture. "Man has it coming to him," he said. "Liquor makes him stupid and he's better off without it. You just leave everything up to me, Mr. Thornton..."

Immediately following breakfast, Frank Seaver stood and, once he'd gotten their attention, told them about a little "entertainment" he had planned. They looked at each other and Po Cartwright shook his head, clearly sensing something afoot that might have unpleasant consequences. But a short time later the six of them gathered by a makeshift range fronting the river. In the interim, Caliban had dragged a log into position and stood before it with a satchel at his feet, awaiting instructions.

Seaver delayed his arrival until everyone was where he wanted them. Waring was hanging on Patricia's arm, plying her with questions, but she kept shaking her head, as baffled as he was. Seaver strode toward them and the transformation was immediately evident; suddenly he had assumed a new and dangerous aspect, menace radiating from him to the extent that all conversation died away as soon as they took notice of his approach.

He was wearing the Colt for the first time in ages and

had to admit it felt good. He'd made no special adaptations to it over the years. Some of his peers made a science out of filing down the big front sight or shortening the barrel (anything to gain the slightest advantage). Others favored gaudy accessories: pearl handles and silver plating. Seaver's pistol sported ordinary black, rubber grips and bore the standard blue, case-hardened finish. No distinguishing features, no notches on the handle.

It ain't the gun, his daddy told him, *it's the man* holdin' *the gun.*

Po Cartwright whistled and mouthed "Lordy, Lordy". Patricia Waring was staring at him but he did his best to shut her out. This show was for her husband, an object lesson and a warning.

"Howdy," he greeted them. "Glad you could make it."

"What is this, Thornton?" Waring snapped, trying to put on a brave front with a swollen head and a hand he still couldn't close properly.

"Well, *Phil,* since you decided to make such a spectacle of yourself yesterday, I thought I'd do the same bright and early this morning."

"So what's your point? To prove you can out-shoot a blind man, is that it?" Waring's tone was mocking. "Yes, well, you'll pardon me if I choose to absent myself from your performance. Come, Patricia." But she resisted, her eyes on Seaver, curious, searching.

"I think you'd better stay right where you are. After all, *you're* the guest of honor."

Waring's face turned bright red. "Shall we dispense with this nonsense? I acknowledge that I—I lost my head last night but I have already made amends with my wife. There's nothing further to—"

"But you didn't make amends with *me*." Seaver's voice, glacially cold and uninflected, drained some of the color from Waring's features. "I took what you said downright personal."

"See here—"

"*Shut up*." Waring twitched. "You won't be able to see much but you got ears and your wife will fill in the rest. Go ahead," he called to Caliban, who nodded and began removing bottles from the satchel, *Waring's entire whiskey stock*, setting them at equidistant points along the length of the log. Meanwhile, Seaver pretended to examine the Colt, spinning the cylinder, playing to his audience. Satisfied, he executed a few twirls before dropping the .45 back into its holster. Fawned watched, her eyes bulging. He resisted an urge to slip her a wink.

Patricia seemed to have withdrawn inside herself, no longer responding to her husband's whispered queries, appearing rather lost and forlorn. He wondered what she was thinking. And if she would ever look at him the same way again.

Caliban finished his preparations, retrieved the empty bag and jogged over to join the rest of them. "All set," he reported, clearly enjoying himself.

"Cal? You're in on this too? I'm disappointed in you, boy." Receiving no reply, Waring blustered on: "What in God's name's gotten into you? Doesn't all I've done for you mean *anything*?"

"Like costing me the use of my arm and treating me like an indentured servant? Your faithful darkie, following his massa around like a common field nigger?" Years of bitterness surged forth, scorn and defiance vying for predominance. "Trading one kind of slavery for another? You can *keep* all the things you've given me, white man.

Take 'em all back. I'm sick to death of you."

Po Cartwright cleared his throat. " 'Fraid that goes for me too, Waring. You can't handle your drink and if yer serious about goin' after that cat, you need a clear head. The whiskey robs you o' your senses and now Frank's gonna make sure what happened last night don't happen again."

"What are you saying?" Waring cried, overwhelmed by the forces allied against him. "What have you done? Cal? Cal? Patricia, for God's sake—"

"Go ahead, Mr. Thornton," the ex-slave urged, "show us what you got."

An *instant* later, the Colt was in his right hand, five lightning fast reports ringing out, echoing in the vastness, man-made thunder. Smoke hung in the air, their ears were still ringing, but already Frank Seaver had swung about and was walking back toward camp.

All five bottles had been obliterated, the air redolent with the stench of cheap alcohol. Fawn was clapping her hands and jumping up and down, but then she paused, puzzled why no one else seemed to have enjoyed the spectacle as much as she had.

Waring was cursing under his breath but, as Po Cartwright remarked to Seaver later, "bein' extra careful not to say nothin' that might cause you offense". Patricia Waring ignored her husband, still trying to come to terms with what she had just seen, a side of the man she knew as "Frank Thornton" that intimidated her, *frightened* her. Her face was wan, colorless. She disengaged from her husband and moved off until she was standing by the riverbank, shoulders slumped. Waring called after her but Cartwright told him to leave her be. "She ain't fit company right now. We'll see you get back all right." He nodded to Fawn, who came over and took Waring's hand.

Waring looked down at her, clearly vexed by the sudden change in his fortunes. "Tell me, Cartwright, you were a witness: was it as impressive as it sounded?"

Cartwright allowed that it was. "I seen my fair share of shootin', men drawin' down on each other, blazin' away. Some of 'em were fast, faster 'n rattlesnakes. But I ain't seen *nothin'* the likes o' that. That was pure spooky was what that was."

Waring nodded glumly. "So...he finally shows his true colors."

Cartwright glared at him. "You wanted a killer, you got one. Jes' don't get it into your head that you can control 'im or treat 'im like some kinda pet. That ain't *never* gonna happen and if you needed proof, I'd say Thornton jes' gave it to you."

"He's a dangerous man."

"Yessir," Po Cartwright confirmed, "and that's why it's a good thing he's on our side. Let's pray it stays that way."

An hour later, Po Cartwright set off alone to see if he could find any indication of the cougar's whereabouts. "Best I go by myself," he explained, "less people the better."

He said a quick farewell to Little Queen and Fawn, then mounted up, pausing as he went past Seaver. "Keep an eye on them clouds yonder," he advised, pointing to the west, "don't like the look of 'em. Dunno about them tents. How they'll hold up. It starts coming down too hard or the wind picks up, grab the horses 'n head for the trees. Leastways they'll give ya shelter. Stay away from the tall ones, though. They attract lightnin'."

"I'll watch the sky," Seaver promised, "meanwhile, *you* worry about that cat."

"Don't concern yourself 'bout that. My ma didn't raise

any fools." He patted his ride affectionately, the animal that so stoically endured his considerable heft. "I see anything with whiskers that ain't a rabbit or coyote, Fred and me'll vamoose damn quick."

"Be sure you do."

Cartwright glanced back toward the others. "Them clouds ain't the only thing you oughta be watchin' out for."

"That so?"

"You showed that man up, showed 'im for what he really is. He ain't liable to forget it."

"I hear you." Seaver held out his hand and they shook on it. "Good huntin', mountain man."

"*Adios*, gunslinger."

He dug his heels into Fred's ample sides and rode away.

Caliban was expecting the weather to turn as well. "Storm headed this way, my arm's hurting like the devil."

"Po said we could use the trees as shelter if we have to."

The black man shrugged. "Sounds good to me. I don't fancy being caught out in the open if a gale starts blowing." He considered the bank of thick, grey clouds. "Probably a couple of hours before it gets here."

"Anythin' we can do in the meantime?"

"There's an extra tarp, we could put that over the Warings' tent. They'd appreciate that." Glancing around the camp. "Maybe get our supplies better stowed. Move the animals so they aren't so exposed. Cover the firewood. That would do for starters."

Seaver nodded. "I'll get everyone pitching in..."

The trees were a mix of aspen, alders and tall, symmetrical conifers tapering to points high above the forest floor. They noted the ones that were older, leaning or stiff with dead wood. Avoided them as they made their storm preparations.

The activity gave them all something to do and helped dispel the lingering tension from the morning. When they encountered each other, Seaver and Waring were civil and, gradually, the atmosphere improved. They worked diligently so that by the time the weather arrived, they were ready for it.

There was surprisingly little rain but the air was super-charged with electricity, a direct result of the recent dry, hot conditions. Jagged lances of lightning leapt through the sky above them, eye-searing jolts that were immediately followed by deafening claps of thunder. The Warings retreated to their tent, while Fawn and Little Queen huddled under a colorful aspen. Occasionally the little girl would cry out in fear, but her mother was there to offer comfort and reassurance.

Seaver and Caliban saw to the animals. They'd strung a good, stout line between some trees and close tethered the horses to it, hobbling them as an added precaution. The two men also rigged blindfolds out of cloth sacks, but the horses remained skittish and they had to work hard to prevent the big animals from panicking and doing injury to their neighbors or themselves.

There were numerous lightning strikes, they could *hear* them, smell the distinctive, metallic whiff of ozone. Three or four came uncomfortably close, one bolt sundering a tree about a hundred yards from where they cowered.

"I hope to God this doesn't cause a fire!" Seaver shouted in the midst of the worst of it.

"You telling me you still believe in God, Mr. Thornton?" Caliban seemed to find the notion quaint.

"You tellin' me right now you *don't*?"

Caliban grinned, a rare display of amusement from the

normally reserved and undemonstrative man.

The storm passed quickly and before long the sun returned, hotter than ever. The ground was soon steaming, the air still and humid. They left the trees and, in short order, restored their former camp. Seaver thought they'd gotten off lucky, until Little Queen discovered nearly a dozen ticks adhering to her daughter and three or four on her own person. He and Caliban looked at each other. "I'll check you if you do the same for me," he offered.

Caliban raised his shoulders in mock resignation. "Won't be the first time I've seen a white man in his natural state..."

It was mid-afternoon when Po Cartwright broke from cover, looking somewhat damp and bedraggled but otherwise no worse for wear. Once he'd dismounted and greeted his family, he turned to Waring, anticipating the inevitable question.

"No sign of our cat but that don't mean he ain't around. I have me a hunch where he might be holed up. Mountain lion like their dens up high and there's a canyon over yonder. I recollect some caves where our critter might be at. I'll give it a look-see come mornin'."

"Is that all?" Waring demanded.

"Nope. Ran into an old pal o' yours, up the trail a ways. That Roosevelt fella. Dude with the glasses—"

"Yes, of course I remember him. What of it?"

"Well, it's jes' that I think you 'n Frank should saddle up and sashay over there. Pay the man a visit."

"What on earth for? Has he seen the cougar?"

"Not so's he mentioned it. Matter o' fact, I'd say yer cat's probably the furthest thing from his mind right about now."

"*What*?" Waring's patience had run its course. "Will

you come to the point, Cartwright?"

"Is he all right?" Seaver asked. He'd grown rather fond of the plucky Yankee.

"Fine 'n dandy. But our ol' lion don't interest him no more. 'Specially now that he's bagged a monster o' his own." Waring gaped at him. "I'd better leave off there. You should hear about it from the man hisself. After all, it's *his* story."

Cartwright and Seaver rode abreast part of the way to Roosevelt's encampment. His companion pointedly eyed the Colt, observing: "Notice you switched shootin' irons. Any perticular reason?"

Seaver was noncommittal. "I like the Colt better."

Cartwright jutted a thumb at Waring, who was content to plod along about ten yards behind them. "Not a-feared he might hold a grudge?"

"My daddy once told me 'turn your back on a man but not on his anger'."

" 'Specially if there's a woman involved," Cartwright added, lowering his voice. Seaver glared at him. "It's plain fact, no use denyin' it. We all can see it. And you can bet yer last nickel *he* can too."

"I think it best you find somethin' else to talk about," Seaver warned. "This subject's worn pretty thin."

"I ain't tryin' to get a rise out o' you, I'm just sayin' it doesn't help the situation. And you got no right to take offense—far as I can see, she's already got a man, which means *yer* the one who's outta line."

Seaver glared at him. "I ain't the only one outta line. And I don't take kindly when someone meddles in my affairs. So be warned, Cartwright. I'm awful quick to bear a grudge."

"Okay, Frank," Cartwright sighed, "it's yer battle so I

guess I'll leave ya to it." He urged Fred forward, leaving Seaver to brood over the exchange. Hard words, but Seaver was an honest man and had to concede there was more truth than fancy to them. Patricia was someone else's woman. That was a fact. He felt Waring's eyes on him, resisted looking back.

Refusing to give him the satisfaction.

Theodore Roosevelt was a man transformed.

Gone was the melancholy he'd borne for so many long months, the deep-seated pain and anger that cast a pall over his every waking hour.

Yet his story, any way you looked at it, was a harrowing one. The man had survived a close brush with death, but rather than bring him low, it had invigorated him, fired him with a renewed sense of purpose and direction.

"There was no warning," he told them, "not the slightest hint that danger lurked nearby." They were ringed about the firepit at the Roosevelt campsite: Seaver, Waring, Cartwright and the entire Roosevelt party. They were a seasoned company by the look of them, among their number Bill Merrifield, Roosevelt's boon companion and right hand man.

The introductions had been perfunctory and no one offered more than a polite greeting. Not an out-going bunch. But they were clearly devoted to their host, regarding him with something akin to awe as he took up his tale.

"It happened less than a mile from where we sit. We were caught off guard and nearly paid for it. It had been a pleasant day in the saddle, the only sound of complaint was from our sore backsides." The remark provoked chuckles. "I was about to suggest that we find a spot to stop for the night, when I was alerted to movement off to the right. An instant later, it burst from the trees, almost as if it had been lying in ambush for us. Bill and I were directly in its path. I had my trusty .45-75 out in case we came across some game for our evening pot. That undoubtedly saved my life."

The bear was enormous, the largest predator Seaver had ever seen. A grizzly that, once extended to its full height, must have stood fully nine feet tall. Perhaps it had been grazing berries or rooting for succulent insects. Then it heard riders approaching—had it ever encountered men before? Certainly it showed no indication of fear as it rushed at them, its speed, for its prodigious size, astonishing. Roosevelt shouted a warning and the grizzly veered, attacking his mount, which reared, spilling its rider to the ground.

With a single swipe of its fearsome claws, the bear disemboweled the unfortunate creature, purple entrails coiling out from a gaping wound in its belly, the animal collapsing in a twitching, shuddering heap.

The rest of the party was in complete disarray, his companions borne off by their terror-stricken horses. No one, it was clear, was in any position to offer assistance to their fallen comrade.

Despite having the wind knocked out of him, Roosevelt retained both his wits *and* his rifle. Once the horse was dealt with, the monstrous grizzly scented *him* and prepared to renew its attack.

"And then, gentlemen, came the moment I shall remember for the rest of my days." Roosevelt's expression revealed equal parts wonder and bafflement. "The beast didn't immediately come for me. There was a moment when we simply regarded each other, two species, face-to-face, about to embark on a struggle to the death." He paused, the emotion the memory inspired still apparent. "I am a man who believes himself to be a servant of Providence. There is an intricate design to the universe, a purpose for every single thing. That bear," nodding at the carcass sprawled a short distance away, "by nearly depriving me of my life, in actuality gave it back to me. For I shall not deceive you: there was a fraction of a second, no more, when I considered lowering my rifle. Tragedy has stolen from me everything I hold dearest and damn near broke me. I have despaired and came close on numerous occasions to giving up and ringing down the curtain on life." His eyes ignited with passion. "But after that briefest of intervals, I brought my Winchester to my shoulder and dispatched the creature without a second thought."

"One shot," Merrifield marveled.

Waring let out his breath. "Well done, Roosevelt," he said. "You are a man of unquestionable valor and fortitude and I salute you!"

Roosevelt was beaming. "I thank you, sir! That is a great compliment, coming from a hunter of your stature."

Po Cartwright rose, went over to the bear, shaking his head at its massive dimensions. "They shore grow 'em big in these parts. This thing's easily over a thousand pounds. Imagine that, half a ton of teeth 'n claws comin' at ya full speed. Lordy..."

"A great land fosters superior creatures," Roosevelt proclaimed. He looked about him. "I could never have imagined such a place. The bounty and diversity of the natural world enlivens the body and soul, enriching our national spirit. We must never allow these sacred groves and peaks to become despoiled by the tawdry reach of modernity."

"You fixin' on runnin fer office again, boss?" One of his cowboy pals joked and Roosevelt chuckled along with the rest of them.

"Cartwright indicated you're considering abandoning your pursuit of the cougar," Waring ventured.

"Indeed. After bagging this rare beast, I feel I have more than achieved my purpose in coming here. It is my intention to pack up and return to my ranch as soon as circumstances allow."

"I applaud your common sense," Waring told him, doing his best to conceal his relief.

"In my view, it would be unsporting to deny you your chance at the cat." Roosevelt offered his hand and Waring took it. "I wish you good hunting, sir."

By the time they took their leave of Theodore Roosevelt, it was getting dark. But it was a clear night, the moon waxing toward fullness and, anyway, there was little likelihood of them getting lost with Cartwright leading the way.

Nonetheless, they kept in close formation, alert for any nocturnal predators that might be lurking about. Surely not another bear but wolves were common to these parts and, of course, the cat had made this *his* hunting ground.

"I like that Roosevelt fella," Cartwright mused at one point. "He's got gumption. The way he faced down that bear...that says somethin' about a man. Tells ya what he's made of."

"Bill Merrifield told me he was some kind of big shot politician back East," Seaver offered. "Said he's the most ambitious man he's ever known."

"Politician, huh? He ain't like any politician *I* ever come across," Cartwright replied and they agreed, to a man, that never were truer words spoken.

CHAPTER TWELVE

CARTWRIGHT LEFT AS SOON as it was light enough, his destination a canyon to the northeast, with caves dotting its granite face. A likely location for their cat.

"I jes' got me a funny feeling that's where the critter's at," was how he put it. "I figger he's a smart one to have lasted this long an' that's one smart place to hole up. An' if he's there, there'll be plenty o' signs."

"Keep your rifle handy," Seaver advised. "That's what saved Roosevelt's hide. You're welcome to my Henry if you like."

Cartwright was tempted but declined the offer. "I been usin' my ol' Hawken so long, it's like part o' my arm." Little Queen packed him a day's worth of food and he hoisted Fawn up for a farewell hug.

"You ain't back by three, we'll come lookin' for you," Seaver said.

"And if you *do* see our lion, Cartwright, I trust you'll restrain yourself from claiming the prize. Your commission is contingent on the premise that *I'm* the one who fires the fatal bullet. Am I clear?

"I'm a man o' my word, Waring," Cartwright growled. "I promised you first crack at the critter and you'll get it. Not that you deserve it..." Before Philip Waring could concoct a rejoinder, Cartwright prodded the bay into a trot, showing him his back.

"I do hope he'll be all right," Patricia Waring fretted. "When I think about Mr. Roosevelt's close call..."

"He knows these mountains, ma'am," Seaver assured her. "That ol' boy can take care of himself, never you fear."

"I'm sure that's the case," she said, sending a small smile his way. It added considerable warmth to a cool-ish, morning...until he noticed the expression on Waring's face. It was an ugly look, wounded and possessive. Seaver found it unsettling. He and the hunter had scrupulously maintained their uneasy truce but it was evident the man still harbored dark thoughts toward him and possibly his wife as well.

While he had previously made allowances for Philip Waring's character defects, now he wasn't nearly as tolerant. His handicap, rather than ennobling him, had left him embittered, suspicious, prone to lashing out at those unfortunate to be in proximity to him...and more often than not it was Patricia who bore the brunt of his hostility. It begged the question: what had their relationship been like *before* his eyes started failing? What had drawn her to him...and how much longer could she endure his mercurial moods?

Seaver was helpless to assist her and yet greatly desired to do something, *anything,* to make her life happier. He cared for her, perhaps even loved her, though he had little experience with matters of the heart. But he had to be careful how he proceeded; Po Cartwright had already divined his feelings and judging from the way Waring was behaving, he wasn't unaware of them either.

Common decency demanded that he render assistance and comfort to a woman of good character and unblemished reputation. Honesty, however, compelled him to acknowledge that his motives, though well-intentioned, weren't entirely selfless.

◆ ◆ ◆

By late morning, the mercury in Philip Waring's thermometer reached eighty-six degrees Fahrenheit. They took their ease as best they could. Fawn and Patricia used the heat as an excuse to wade into the river, splashing and gamboling in the shallows.

Waring, somehow alerted that Seaver was in the process of saddling the Nag, made his way over to where the animals were tethered, using his cane to probe his way along. He must have been either too timid or too stubborn to ask anyone to assist him.

"Going somewhere?"

Seaver reached underneath, cinching the saddle to the Nag's mid-section, tugging it good and tight. "Figured I'd see if there's any game about. We lost some of our meat supply when that packhorse fell. The gals are great at gathering mushrooms but a man can't live on that. Not this man, anyway. If I were you," he added, noticing the Nag's ears flattened back, "I'd hold it right there. This horse of mine is fixin' to take a bite outta you. Critter is partial to neither man nor beast."

Waring halted. "Is that why you keep him away from the rest?"

"Can't trust him, never know what he's liable to do. And he don't usually give any warning either, that's why I told you to watch yourself."

"Yet he seems to tolerate you. You should call him Bucephalus."

"Wasn't that Alexander the Great's horse?"

Waring was surprised. "You know the story?"

Seaver paused, looked over his shoulder at him. "I like readin'. You want somethin'?"

Waring seemed discomfited by the question. "I'm ...somewhat bored. I'd like to accompany you, if you're amenable. I can have Cal saddle my horse and be ready in no time."

Seaver wasn't enamored with the notion but couldn't think of a way of begging off that wouldn't run the risk of offending him. "I got no objection. Just don't get between me and some big, fat turkey."

Seaver completed his preparations, checked his ammo and decided to take the opportunity to fill his canteen with fresh water. He walked down to the river and was greeted by Patricia and Fawn.

"Come to cool off?" This from the former.

He held up the canteen. "Need a refill." He knelt and submerged it in the cold, clear stream. With his free hand, he cupped some water, splashed it on his face and the nape of his neck. Chilly beads slid down his back, cooling as they went. When the canteen was full, he wandered over to join them.

Fawn, lacking any sense of propriety, had shed most of her clothing and seemed better off for it. Patricia retained her modesty, her one accommodation removing her boots and stockings, exposing her ankles and calves. She lolled on the pebbled bank, her feet submerged in the frigid stream.

There was nothing provocative about her pose, yet the sight of her bare legs stirred something inside him and he had to look away. But then he was drawn to her face, angled toward the sun, her hair unclipped, falling in loose curls. He was captivated, hardly trusting himself to speak.

"You, uh, wanna be careful, ma'am," he told her, "at this altitude the sun's extra hot. Gotta watch you don't get yourself a nasty burn."

She sighed. "I suppose you're right." She nodded toward Fawn, crouched in the water, trying to catch minnows with her nimble hands. "Doesn't she make you envious? So carefree."

"She's lucky. All that dirt will help keep the sun off her. It's like wearin' an extra layer of bear grease."

She laughed. "Perhaps it's a lesson for all of us. Sometimes good hygiene has its drawbacks." They heard a horse approaching, turned simultaneously.

"Shall we go, Thornton?" Waring must have known his wife was there, yet he didn't so much as nod in her direction. She appeared unconcerned, barely registering his presence. Strange...

"Good day to you, ma'am. Remember what I said about the sun." But she had returned her attention to the river, waving at Fawn, giggling at her antics. Waring jerked his horse's reins, wrenching its neck and causing it to lurch awkwardly. Then he was steering it away, digging his spurs in, a cruel and needless display of pique.

Seaver thought, *that man is a fool and a tyrant and one day, God willing, he'll get his proper comeuppance.*

He only hoped the punishment fit the crime.

Once they moved into the trees the ferocity of the sun's rays was greatly diminished. The shade brought welcome relief and helped improve Seaver's disposition. Having Waring along was an annoyance but he was getting over it. At least his companion didn't appear to be in a talkative mood, which was a welcome change.

They picked their way through the woods, following old, meandering animal trails, Seaver remaining vigilant, hoping to startle a deer or other edible varmint into the open. Every so often he would check Waring but was continually impressed by how well he navigated the woody maze. His horse was an able accomplice, superb at evading the worst of the obstructions and impediments.

"That sure is one well-trained animal you got there."

"It should be," came Waring's uncharitable reply, "I paid enough for the damn thing."

Seaver thought it best to make no further comment.

They flushed some small game and Seaver shot two sizable hares, a fat quail and a black-tailed mule deer they discovered drinking at a spring a mile or so from camp. It didn't take flight when they came into view and Seaver brought it down from his saddle, the Nag considerately staying still long enough for him to get off his shot.

He was in the process of securing the muley to his mount when he heard Waring chamber a round into his rifle, an ominous, metallic *clack*.

"Big cats and humans have a number of things in common, did you know that, Thornton? First of all, we're natural born killers. It's our nature to consume lesser creatures than ourselves. But another trait we share is that we're both highly territorial creatures and we protect what's ours with pure, animal savagery."

"Is that a fact?" Seaver angled his body until he was facing the mounted man, his left hand still on his saddle horn, his right resting on the butt of the Colt.

Waring's Winchester carbine was at his shoulder, cocked and aimed directly at him. He was only twelve feet away; from that position it was unlikely he'd miss. The bullet would either kill Seaver or cause considerable damage. Neither outcome was particularly attractive.

He made a conscious effort to quiet his breathing. There had been a jolt of adrenaline when he realized the hunter had the drop on him but no fear, only disappointment that he'd allowed himself get caught with his pants down.

"Personally, I'm *very* territorial, especially when it

comes to my wife."

"What's she got to do with this?" Seaver blurted, cursing himself, for the muzzle, which had been wandering off target, found him again.

"You know exactly what I mean, you *bastard*." Waring's voice shook with rage and once again the rifle twitched, the beaded Freund sight now centered on a spot high on Seaver's right shoulder. "You both think I'm stupid. My eyes may be going but, I told you, my ears have adapted beautifully and I can hear the way her heart beats faster when she's around you. Even her *smell* changes, like a cat in heat."

Seaver's fury boiled over. "You foul-mouthed son of a bitch. That woman hasn't done anything to cause you to behave like this. She's beautiful, there's no use denyin' it, but she's as honest and loyal as the day is long. You married her, surely you must know that."

"You must take me for a fool," Waring sneered. "The two of you sneaking off together as soon as my back is turned. Well, I won't have it! I won't have you carrying on in front of the others, in front of that no good nigger. You hear?" The muzzle of the rifle looked as big as a silver dollar. All Waring had to do was put the slightest pressure on the trigger to inflict serious injury or death. "Not so smart now, are you, Thornton? Not when you're facing a *real* man and staring death in the eye. You got anything to say before I send your soul to hell where it belongs?"

"Yeah. You should lower your aim some. Right now, you're way too high. You're liable to just wing me. And that wouldn't be good." Waring was dumbfounded, unsure how to react. "Go on, do as I say. Down a bit and to your right. Otherwise you'll only hit my shoulder. Bad enough, but probably not gonna kill me, even from that range. You wanna make sure and that means a chest shot. Anything else and I'll be alive and then you won't be, I promise you that. Come on, Waring, you're still off target! Now you're shaking, that's only gonna make it *worse*." The hunter was sweating heavily and it wasn't just the heat of the day. "You're wandering again," Seaver taunted him. "Damnit, man, what's wrong with you? Hold it steady...steady, I said!"

Waring groaned. "*Damn* you, Thornton..."

"Shut up." He was seething. "You shoot animals but *I'm* a man-killer, understand? You think I ain't faced death before? You think somethin' like this is gonna *break* me?" He chuckled, a low, harsh sound. "Not hardly. You got the drop on me but that don't mean nothin'. Not until you pull that trigger. Only then will your troubles will be over."

"What are you *saying*?" Philip Waring's voice cracked, hysteria leaking through. "I'll kill you, I swear I will! I'll never let you take her from me! What's mine is mine."

"Then *pull*, you bastard. But know this: *I'll see it*. I'll see the thought form in your mind. And even as it's bein' born, before it has a chance to make it to your finger, *I'll kill you*. You know how fast I am. As sure as the sun rises, I will put you in the ground."

Waring's eyes bugged out at him, not sightless now, seeing his own end, bullets ripping into his flesh, watching himself thrown from his horse, blood blooming from his torso, staining the forest floor. Seaver saw his fear and uncertainty, the dawning realization that events had spiraled out of his control and now *he* was the one under penalty of death, not his antagonist. Seaver's hand hovered over the Colt, waiting for a tremor, a *tic*, the most subtle indication that his opponent had recovered his nerve. He had every intention of killing the man, there wasn't the slightest doubt that in the next few seconds he would do what his instincts and character demanded.

"You...you..." It appeared Waring had lost his bloodlust. He was blinking rapidly, sweat stinging his eyes, the gun drooping, no longer a viable threat.

"Make your move. I'm waiting. I figure I'll gut shoot you, leave you to the animals. Maybe another bear like the one that nearly got Roosevelt—"

Waring threw back his head, howling, simultaneously raising his carbine into the air and discharging the round in its chamber. In two strides, Seaver was beside him, reaching up and wrenching him off his horse. Waring lost his footing but Seaver immediately hauled him upright and slapped him, a skull-rattling blow.

"So you're stupid *and* you're yellow. It's good I found that out. A man needs to know the kind of people he's dealin' with. What happened to you, Waring? You used to be something, you used to have *guts*. Now look at you." Seaver shook him until his teeth rattled, then slung him to the ground in disgust.

"Damn you," he sobbed, "you don't know what it's like."

"I know one thing," Seaver said. "You don't deserve that woman. You ain't man enough for her. Now get on your damn horse and get the hell outta my sight. You make me sick just lookin' at you." He retrieved Waring's rifle, ejected the rest of the cartridges, rammed it into its scabbard. Stalked over to the Nag, swung up into the saddle and rode away.

Leaving him there...

"Where's Waring?" Po Cartwright reached up, gripped his arm. "You didn't—"

"No, but I came damn close." With a sigh of relief,

Cartwright fell in step beside him. "He's somewhere behind me. I figured his horse was smart enough to find the way back even if he wasn't." He climbed down and walked the Nag over to where he was kept tethered. Those horses nearest nickered nervously, sidling out of the way.

"So the two of you finally got into it." Cartwright tugged at his beard in agitation. "You jes' had that look about you. That's why I figgered you kilt him."

"I sure as hell thought about it. Bastard pulled on me when my back was turned. For a second I thought he might have it in him to do it but I guess he changed his mind."

"Lucky for you."

"Lucky for *him*. I'd have killed him in a heartbeat and he knew it. Man plain lost his nerve."

"Well, he'd better git it back again durn quick 'cause I think I found his cougar."

"Was it where you thought?"

"Yep." Cartwright thumped his chest. "Me heap good scout."

Seaver grinned. "You done your part. I guess the rest is up to him."

"Yeah. But the question is, is our great white hunter up to it? If he's as bad off as you say—"

"See for yourself. Here he comes now."

"Let's jes' pray you haven't cost me my commission. That would jes' about ruin my cheerful disposition." Philip Waring emerged from the woods and his posture, the way he carried himself, revealed the depths to which he had sunk. Cartwright whistled. "That man looks plain whupped."

"He got what was coming to him," Seaver said, slipping the saddle off and then the wool underblanket, damp with sweat. Someone, most likely Caliban, had fetched fresh water and the Nag already had his nose stuck in the bucket. Then it commenced tearing into the nearest patch of bunchgrass, chewing contentedly.

"Afternoon, Mr. Waring," Cartwright called, going over to meet him. "Lemme get your horse for you." He held the animal while Waring climbed down. "Out huntin', were you?"

"What have you got for me?" Waring demanded, his voice raspy. "Come on, Cartwright, I haven't got all day."

"What I got is good news," Cartwright explained, ignoring his foul mood. "I took a gander at that box canyon I tol' you about. I was right, there's caves galore and I spotted tracks, some bones too, lotsa scat. Whatever's up there is big and it *ain't* a bear."

"Anything else?"

"Not really. It'll depend on the wind but we should be able to get pretty close. Find what path it uses, set ourselfs up nice and pretty and wait for it to show itself."

"We'll go first thing tomorrow, find out if your hunch is right."

"Oh, I'm right. I *feel* it. It's there, waitin' for us. For *you*, that is."

"So you say." Waring's tone abrupt, dismissive.

Cartwright's face darkened. "That's right. That's what I say. I found him and now the question is, are you up to the job of goin' and *gettin'* him?"

Waring started toward him, purpling with fury. "Up to—why, *you*—"

"Careful, Waring," Seaver advised, "I don't think you wanna make *two* new enemies today."

Waring's mouth clamped shut and he spun about, stomping off in a huff. But the toe of one of his boots caught in a hole, maybe an old ground squirrel den, and he stumbled. Enraged, he limped away, bawling for his wife or Caliban, neither of whom seemed to be within earshot. He staggered along, arms flung out before him, until at last he managed to find his tent, angrily throwing open the front flap and crawling inside.

CHAPTER THIRTEEN

IN THE MORNING, soft whorls of mist floated above the river and a fresh sheen of dew covered the grass and bullrushes, sparkling on their bedclothes and beading on the bodies of the dozing animals.

While the rest stamped their feet and moved about, trying to get their blood flowing again, Little Queen prepared a simple, hardy breakfast, feeding thin strips of venison into a heavy, cast iron pan that constituted a deadly weapon, at least in her hands.

The atmosphere was strained, the solidarity of the group sorely tested by inner divisions and growing animosity toward the man who had set events in motion and brought them to this juncture. There were very few words exchanged and Waring sat alone on one side of the fire, his mood pensive, thoughts inwardly turned.

As soon as they'd eaten, Frank Seaver rose and pronounced himself ready. "Gonna be a good day for it, by the looks of it," he observed.

"Some weather later though," Caliban, rubbing his arm. "By suppertime, I'd say."

"That arm ever wrong?"

Caliban shrugged. "Not usually."

"I'll take your word for it. How far away did you say this canyon is, Po?"

"A hour and some. I might know a shortcut."

"Sounds good. Just don't make it too strenuous, I ain't as young as I used to be." Seaver paused. "I ain't too happy about leaving the women here on their own but I don't see any choice." Glancing at Caliban. "You're his spotter, you're the one that tells him where to shoot." Turning to Waring. "We'll get you as close as we can and the first shot is yours. You miss and—"

"No need to belabor the point," Waring said, his voice flat, monotonic. All the fight gone out of him.

"It's still your show. But that thing poses a threat to any of us, we'll put it down for you. You're welcome to its hide, but it ain't welcome to *ours'*. Got it?"

Waring's face looked bleak. His wife had not seen fit to rise and see him off and there had been little contact between them for the previous few days. Caliban performed his duties with his usual diligence but his disdain for his employer was obvious. This journey had cost Philip Waring a great deal, did he still think it was worth the accompanying hardship and sacrifice?

The four men rode out single file, their thickset guide at the head of the abbreviated column. Cartwright was adamant that Little Queen was more than up to the task of protecting the camp against any peril, human or otherwise, during their absence. "She's better with a rifle or knife than I am," he boasted. "Ain't nothin' that walks 'r crawls puts the fright into her."

Seaver believed him.

Cartwright's shortcut took them through an open patch of prairie and then into the woods, a dim trek, the trees pressing in on every side, the path undifferentiated, confusing to everyone except the man in front. Seaver gave up trying to identify telltale landmarks that would help him retrace his steps, putting his faith in Cartwright's abilities and instincts. They came out of the woods and followed a stream into a small, secluded corridor enclosed by sharp, piney bluffs. Then they were climbing. At times it was a steep ascent, loose rocks clattering around them, cascading all the way to the bottom. On several occasions they had to dismount and lead their horses, the terrain making no allowance for man or beast.

And yet animal life was abundant here. Everywhere they passed, there were holes and warrens for burrowers, old fox or coyote dens, short barks and chirrups communicating the presence of *strangers*, keeping track of their progress. Overhead, hawks and eagles wheeled and soared, alert for prey. Ducks and geese were also in evidence, drawn to the plentiful water, their calls resembling far-off laughter. Raucous and mocking.

"This is quite the country," Seaver panted at one point, glancing back in time to see Philip Waring stumble, almost losing his grip on the reins. "Careful there, Phil!" He called out maliciously. "You fall and you're liable to keep goin'." Waring waved him off.

"Wouldn't be no loss," Caliban grunted. Not caring if anyone heard him.

"This is the worst bit," their guide assured them, "once we reach the top it flattens out again."

"Thank God for small favors," Seaver said. "This ol' cowboy ain't used to all this leg work."

While they waited for Waring, Po Cartwright made a slow turn, taking in their surroundings. "I do love this place. I can't never get enough of it. I been around, seen some amazing sights but...nothin' like this." Waring caught up with them, looking scuffed and disheveled. "I tell you, lads, if God still walks the earth, I guarantee He spends a considerable amount of time here, eyeballin' the scenery."

Caliban listened, his expression skeptical, but said nothing.

Cartwright's words proved prophetic: soon they were back on their horses and not long afterward he announced they were nearing their destination. "Pretty quick we'll get off and walk again. We can't leave the horses, our cat ain't the only critter in these parts."

"Will it be around this time of day?" Seaver inquired. "Won't it be out huntin'?"

Cartwright pondered the query. "Hard to know. Some cats do their huntin' by day, some at night. There's no way of tellin' 'til we take a look-see."

"In Africa, the big cats rest in the heat of the day, preserving their energy. It's after dark when they're most dangerous. I can still picture their eyes, shining like fireflies." It was the longest sentence Philip Waring had uttered all day. "You remember, Cal?"

"I remember." The recollection clearly gave the black man little pleasure. Not the sentimental type.

"Well, this is the Yellowstone and I'll be keepin' my Hawken handy, just in case."

Waring merely shrugged, signifying agreement or indifference, it was hard to tell which.

A few minutes later, Cartwright signaled for them to dismount. They moved cautiously, making as little noise as possible. Seaver held the Nag's reins while keeping his right hand free. His gun hand.

At one point Cartwright paused, checking, then: "Damn. We're upwind. That ain't good but nothin' we can do about it. It's these mountains, swirlin' everthin' around." He spat and continued on.

If Cartwright's hunch was correct, the cat's den was one in a series of caves and niches carved by the agents of time in a rocky canyon a few hundred yards away. They crept closer, convening in a narrow ravine, huddling around

Cartwright.

He kept his voice low. "This is right around where I found the signs. There's an elk carcass, yonder." Pointing. "Big one too." He set a heavy rock on his horse's reins and the others did the same, Caliban wordlessly assisting his employer. Brandishing the Hawken, Cartwright led the way, the other three falling in behind. At one point Waring stumbled, cursing, and Caliban instinctively reached out and took his arm, guiding him. Cartwright frowned at the racket but said nothing. Suddenly, he stopped. Kneeling, he beckoned for them to join him. "Take a look at this. C'mere, Waring." Caliban led him to where the guide was squatting. "Hunker down here—that's right. Now gimme yer mitt." Cartwright guided his hand into an impression left in the thin layer of soil. "You see that?"

"Good God," was the best Waring could manage.

"Jes' about your whole hand fits in there." He leaned back. "What do ya say? What kinda animal leaves a print like that?"

"Remarkable." He took a deep breath. "It's even larger than I dared imagine."

"You sure we got enough guns?" Caliban murmured and Cartwright nodded.

"I'm startin' to wonder that myself."

Waring seemed in a daze. "It's...extraordinary. I can hardly credit such a thing is possible."

"Oh, it's possible. Remember that bear yer pal Roosevelt kilt? This is wild country, boys. Long before our kind walked the earth, these big critters hunted and bred and in all that time they've known no fear because there was nothin' *to* fear. To them, our kind is jes' meat. That bear wasn't afraid of him and why should it be? It's never come across anything bigger or meaner and jes' took it for granted that it had every right to do what it did. And who are we to say it was wrong?"

Seaver nodded. "Any idea how big this thing is, Po?"

"At least nine feet, includin' the tail. See the size of the pad? That's yer measurin' stick. And look at the depth of the print. Bastard's two hunnerd pounds, likely more. There's somethin' else too." He traced the outline of the impression with his finger. "This is recent, *real* recent. See how the edges crumble? It ain't had time to set. And that ain't exactly comfortin', if y'all get my meaning."

Caliban glanced around apprehensively. "I don't know about you gentlemen, but right now I'm beginning to wonder if we're up to this. Perhaps we should withdraw and consider another—"

"But we're *men*," Waring spoke up, "we have superior brains, the ability to reason. And weapons, weapons that can kill at a distance, with little risk to ourselves. No, I simply refuse to assign any great power or significance to this beast. It is merely a larger version of its species. It's admirable, perhaps, that it has survived this long, surprising in light of the rigors of the natural world. *But it's only an animal* and animals are subordinate to mankind, that is the natural order of things as it was ordained long, long ago."

"I surely hope yer right about that," Cartwright said. " 'Cause this here print ain't from long ago. Mebbe only a few *hours* ago. Somethin' could be up there right now, watchin' us, makin' its own plans. We'd better pray it's got sense enough to know jes' how much smarter and superior we are."

Seaver crouched down beside Cartwright. "How do you want to handle this, Po? What's your plan?"

"First, we arm ourselves to the teeth. Then we gotta hope this wind shifts or dies down. Otherwise, he's sure to nose us out. From what I can tell, this is the way he usually takes to his huntin' ground. So we'll squirrel ourselfs away somewhere and wait 'im out."

"Sounds good to me." The scheme seemed to satisfy the others as well.

"He's either up there already or out prowlin'. Either way, he'll have to pass by here to get where he's goin'. Could be he's got a back door, but we'll worry 'bout that later. We'll try this first, see what happens."

They moved their horses to a better location and found themselves a vantage point offering both concealment and a modicum of shade from the scorching sun. They observed strict silence now, communication, when necessary, conducted *via* nudges and nods.

Waring seemed largely unaware of the others. His rifle of choice, a custom Sharps fitted with special sights, was propped across his knees and his posture gave the impression that even had his vision miraculously returned, he would have taken little notice of those around him. Perhaps he was ruminating on other hunts, other vigils, finding a still center in his being while waiting for his quarry to show itself. How many hours had he spent, patient as a stone, biding his time, alert for any movement or stealthy footfall. Primed to kill.

But today was not his day.

Cartwright waited until mid-afternoon before suggesting they quit their location and resume the stakeout on the morrow. He'd been watching the sky with growing trepidation. Dark clouds descending, moving inexorably in their direction. "Don't like the look o' that, boys. We'd better get ourselfs in the saddle and on our way, 'less we wanna end up drowned in our boots."

Seaver had to admit weather conditions looked especially

threatening and seconded the decision to call it a day. Even if they made haste it was unlikely they'd make it back before the storm broke. Waring and Caliban made it unanimous.

They grabbed their gear and hurried to the horses, Caliban shepherding his employer and not being too conscientious about it, Seaver noted. There was plenty of stumbling and muttered curses along the way. Two old companions, now fallen out and thoroughly disenchanted with each other.

On the return trip, Po Cartwright led the way once again, with Seaver last one in line. He had little to do except keep an eye on Philip Waring, make sure some perfectly placed branch didn't unceremoniously unhorse him. But he needn't have bothered; Waring seemed much restored, sitting straighter in the saddle and taking an active interest in his surroundings, what he could detect with his weak eyes. He was largely oblivious to the banter of the other men, too preoccupied with navigating the difficult trail to contribute much to the conversation. On several occasions he anticipated upcoming changes in their route, calling out to Cartwright for confirmation—he was right every time. For a man with lousy peepers, he had a superb sense of direction.

The clouds raced overhead, unleashing their burden when the four were still a good distance from their destination. This time there *was* rain, and plenty of it, along with strong winds that lashed the treetops above them. They had some measure of protection from the worst of it but by the time they emerged from the woods and made a final dash to the campsite, they were drenched to the bone.

Little Queen, assisted by Patricia Waring and Fawn, had done a first class job weatherproofing the camp. The loose gear was stowed and extra canvas had been lashed over the Warings' tent. They'd also erected a modest "A" tent, of sufficient size to accommodate four or five sleepers, in a pinch. It was well staked and secure against all but the strongest gales.

The horses were quickly dealt with, the hunters separating, Waring and Caliban retreating to their respective tents, Seaver joining Cartwright's people in the communal tepee. The rain persisted, drumming on the canvas structure with impressive force. Thunder rumbled and boomed, accompanied by blue-white bolts of lightning that illuminated their surroundings with flashes of searing brilliance.

"What a country," Po Cartwright complained from one dark corner. "Boils you alive by day and drowns you at night." Seaver laughed. Fawn and Little Queen were curled up under the buffalo robe, deaf to the storm, dead to the world.

It had been a long day and soon Seaver found himself dozing as well. He jolted awake and wondered aloud if someone should go out and check the horses, but Cartwright volunteered that the weather was the best sentry they could ask for. "Nothin' movin' out there and horses won't stray far in *that*," he said, referring to the downpour. "Best get some sleep. You'll be needin' yer wits come mornin'."

After that, Seaver gave no further thought to the matter, falling into a deep slumber. A dreamless, satisfying sleep, disregardful of the angry sky, leaky roof and close proximity of his companions.

With the arrival of dawn, however, he was abruptly awakened by shrill, anguished cries from outside. It was Patricia Waring and something was terribly wrong...

"He's gone!"

She was frantic, running toward them as they emerged from their soggy shelter, seeking to discover the cause of her distress.

Once they got her calmed down it quickly became apparent what had transpired. Philip Waring had left their shared tent at some point during the night, waiting until the storm had shown signs of abating. His wife was vaguely aware of his departure but thought little of it at the time, assuming that he was stepping out to answer nature's call and would soon return. Waking some hours later, however, she was alarmed to find him *still* missing and unable to discover his whereabouts despite a thorough search of the camp.

The storm had conspired to cover his movements and, too, the rest of the company had slept so deeply it likely would've taken a cavalry charge, bugles blaring, to stir them.

Waring's horse was missing, his Sharps rifle as well. Caliban shook his head. "That is one fool of a white man."

"You figger he went after the cat?" Po Cartwright called over to Seaver as they saddled their respective mounts.

"Don't you?"

Cartwright grimaced. "He's got a good head start. Although how he'll find that canyon all by his lonesome—"

Seaver groaned as it came to him. "He'll find it. I saw him yesterday and it was like he was bein' extra watchful. Payin' attention where we were goin'. Remember how he knew when we were turnin'? Those weren't just lucky guesses, he somehow *saw* it in his head. The smart son of a bitch..."

Cartwright was gaping at him. "Could he do that? I mean...it don't seem possible."

"Sure he could. He's always braggin' about how he's got extra sharp senses now that his eyes are shot. And don't forget that horse of his. You've seen the way it's trained. How it knows when to—"

Little Queen hollered something, gesticulating toward the trees.

Philip Waring's horse had appeared and was trotting toward them.

Of its rider, however, there was no sign.

They just about had to hogtie Patricia Waring to keep her from coming with them. As it was, Caliban was barely able to restrain her, half-carrying, half-dragging her away, Little Queen and Fawn following along, trying to console her.

"I'm startin' to like that darkie," Cartwright admitted, as they rode away together. "He ain't such a bad sort."

"People are the same inside, black or white," Seaver offered.

"And jes' as liable to be fools," Cartwright concluded, urging Fred into a ragged canter.

The pair retraced their journey of the previous day, sharp-eyed in case Waring had merely tumbled from his horse and was lying beside the track, dead or insensible. But as the morning wore on it became more and more evident that scenario was not the one being played out.

"I'm gettin' a funny kinda feelin', Frank."

"I know. This ain't gonna come out well. Maybe it never was."

Cartwright looked over his shoulder at him. "Not sure what you mean by that."

"We'll just wait and see," was all Seaver would say.

They found what was left of Philip Waring near the location where they'd waited for the cougar. Cartwright saw him first and barked an angry epithet. Seaver pulled up alongside and the two of them gazed down at the mound of shredded rags and torn flesh lying a short distance away.

"Ah, damn him. Damn him and his foolish notions and stupid pride." Cartwright groaned. "Lordy. What a terrible, terrible thing." They dismounted and approached the butchered remains with little enthusiasm. "You can see where he was dragged." Pointing out the trail of blood. "It got him there, where the ground's all trampled…" Looking at Seaver, mystified. "This don't make sense. He come out o' hiding—he *showed* hisself! If he'd just waited where he was, he coulda—"

"Po." Interrupting the tirade. "There's no rifle."

"Huh?"

"Look around you," Seaver told him. "It ain't here."

Cartwright searched the area near the body. "Mebbe it's under him."

"No. I think he left it back there. C'mon." Sure enough, they found the Sharps propped against a stone outcropping, dry and clean and unfired. Po Cartwright commenced cursing again but Seaver put a hand on his shoulder, squeezing for emphasis. "C'mon now. This ain't the time for dolin' out blame. Let's get our shovels and do right by him. We ain't takin' him back to his wife lookin' like that."

"You knew, didn't you?" Cartwright accused him. "Knew we'd find him like this."

"I reckon he got the idea from Roosevelt. When he told us about how when that big grizzly came at him, he almost let it take him. How tempted he was. Or maybe Waring had it in mind all along. I guess we'll never know."

"But it's *us* left cleanin' up the mess. Buryin' him and then havin' to go back and tell his pretty wife what he's gone and done."

"No." He held Cartwright's gaze. "The cat got him, plain

and simple. He got off a shot, put up a terrible fight, but in the end it was too much for him."

"You think he deserves that?"

"Probably not. But *she* does."

Together, they hacked out a depression in the stony ground, aided, to some extent, by the overnight rainfall. They worked silently, occasionally helping each other pry out an obstructing rock, pausing every so often to wipe the sweat from their brows. Then they set about gathering the heaviest stones and stacking them in a pile by the grave.

"Now comes the hard part," Cartwright sighed. "Jes' tell yourself it ain't a man. Hell, we're all just meat and bones, once ya strip the skin off."

"Is that supposed to make me feel better?"

They dragged and shoveled and scraped Waring's body into the hole they'd made for him. There were no words spoken, nothing sacred implied. Once they were satisfied they'd done all they could, they filled in the trench and piled rocks on top of it. No grave marker, no memorial. Eventually weather and time would erase all evidence of their efforts, dust returning to dust.

It was done.

No. Not quite. Po Cartwright retrieved a leather pouch from his saddlebag. He shook out a small amount of black powder, poured it on to a flat rock on the burial mound. Striking a match, he put it to the powder, causing it to flare up, releasing an acrid, sulfurous cloud. Nodding in satisfaction. "Old custom," he mumbled by way of explanation, "s'posed to keep the varmints away."

They looked at each other, sweaty, sore, calluses leaking, backs aching. Reached across the simple cairn and gripped hands.

Then Cartwright saw something over Seaver's shoulder

and his mouth fell open, eyes widening to comic proportions. Surprise and shock contorted his features. He tried to say something but it came out wrong, nonsense syllables. Finally managed to blurt: "Frank... Lordy...*look*!

He turned slowly, one hand on the Colt, braced for trouble.

The cougar had paused partway up the slope and was staring down at them. Even from a hundred yards away the details were clear and sharp. Seaver could see that the cat was in the prime of life, its tan coat immaculate, tautly stretched across its long, lithe frame.

Cartwright's estimates of its size were close but didn't do justice to the grace, majesty and primal energy the cougar exuded. Its gaze revealed an utter lack of fear or agitation. The creature's mouth and whiskers were stained with Waring's blood, its stomach full and distended. Cartwright was muttering something under his breath in a tongue unfamiliar to Seaver. A prayer, in any language.

Their rifles were propped only a few steps away and, who knows, they might have gotten off one or two shots before it leaped and scrambled to safety.

Neither of them moved.

The seconds stretched out, an interval during which the world around them seemed suspended in a middle distance, beyond time and space, far removed from familiar places and comforting routine.

Then, from overhead, the irate screech of some bird of prey broke the spell. They glanced up simultaneously, only for a split second...but it was long enough. When they looked again, the cougar was gone.

"I wanted to kill it," Po Cartwright whispered. "But I...I..."

"He belongs here, Po, not us. *We're* the intruders. This

is his land, his home. And we should leave him to it." Seaver patted his shoulder. "C'mon, mountain man, let's head back. There ain't nothin' left for us here."

They walked slowly toward their horses, steeling themselves for what came next.

CHAPTER FOURTEEN

PATRICIA WARING HAD barely spoken since her husband's death.

She shunned company, plodding along behind the others, vacant-eyed, indifferent to the rest of the world. She didn't refuse food but left most of it on her plate, uneaten. Fawn sometimes managed to connect with her, holding her hand, smiling up at her, but such moments were sporadic and fleeting. For the most part, she gave back nothing.

On the return journey they stayed at some of their old camp sites but there was no sense of nostalgia, only a desire to hasten back to Livingston with all due speed. The mood was morose and it affected everyone. Po Cartwright and Little Queen bickered constantly over trivial matters and vented their anger on poor Fawn, admonitions doled out in three different languages.

Seaver finally took pity on the kid, motioning for her to ride with him and leave her parents to their squabbling. She welcomed the offer and they rode together for some hours, rarely exchanging more than the occasional shy smile or nod, but enjoying the company.

"The Queen's mad at me," Cartwright told him one afternoon, glancing around to make sure no one else was in the vicinity. "An Injun through and through, that woman. Says if the wife won't pay us, we should take their gear, either use it or sell it. I told her to simmer down and she jes' about run me through with that pig-sticker she totes 'round with her." He pulled at his beard, something he did habitually whenever he was nervous or anxious. Or both. "It's all Waring's fault. If he'd acted like a man, instead of—"

"Let's not go into that, Po. Wait 'til we get back to town. And you can tell that squaw of yours if Pat—*Mrs. Waring* ain't in any shape to cover your expenses, I'll make up the difference out of my own pocket. Don't worry, I'm good for it."

"Naw, naw," vehemently shaking his shaggy head, "that wasn't what I was gettin' at."

"Never mind. Just leave the widow be, at least until we hit Livingston. You'll get your money, don't fret on that account."

"Aw, now, don't be sore, Frank..."

By that point, Seaver was fed up with the lot of them. Things had come to a bad end and there didn't seem to be any way to make it better. Could he have changed the sequence of events, saved Waring from himself? Probably not. Had he *wanted* to? That was another question. The woman had turned his head and foolish pride had done the rest.

As the days passed, he devoted a significant portion of time to berating himself for the passivity and conceit that had led to this dire outcome. He'd watch her horse amble by, see Patricia's pale, blank face and feel a renewed surge of guilt and responsibility, a lingering shame that the passage of time did not diminish.

At last, he sought out Caliban, who had been tending to her as best he could, his devotion patient and unstinting.

"She blames herself," the black man explained, clearly bewildered by her reasoning. "Near the end, they hadn't been on speaking terms. There's been trouble between them before and it usually had to do with his drinking."

"Tell you the truth, I didn't much care for him *sober*."

Caliban shrugged. "He changed in the last while, got meaner. Not saying he was perfect before but you saw him at his worst. Going blind finished him. It unmanned him, took away everything that made him who he was."

"What will she do now?"

"Don't think she knows herself. Eight years she was with him, seen him through thick and thin. And now she thinks she betrayed him, somehow made him do what he did. Like he had to *prove* something to her by killing that cat."

"She's wrong, Cal. The man had a death wish, plain and simple."

"Nothing's that simple," Caliban replied. "Her husband's dead and she's alone. Not only that, her mind has turned against her. What happens next...well, your guess is as good as mine."

Seaver had been brooding over that conversation ever since. Now they were less than a day from their destination and the time had come to do what he should've done a lot sooner.

He got his opportunity when they stopped for lunch in Paradise Valley.

Patricia, as was her habit of late, ate little. Giving Fawn her plate, she left them, wading into an adjoining field of wild daisies and vivid, purple fireweed. Facing south, the direction from which they'd come; returning to the scene of her crime. Gusts of wind created wave-like effects in the surrounding meadow, heaves and swells eddying about her, threatening to overwhelm her in a sea of bright blooms. Every so often, she would reach down and brush the tips of the flowers with her fingers, an aimless gesture that said much about her state of mind.

"Like to have a word with you if I could, ma'am." He

saw her shoulders stiffen and when she turned, her face retained its mask-like appearance, forbidding and remote.

"Please, Mr. Thornton, I'd like to be left alone."

"That may be but there ain't likely to be another chance to say some things that need to be said." She closed her eyes, lowering her head. "I know you're carryin' around a terrible burden. All of us can see how you're blamin' yourself for what happened and that ain't right."

"My feelings are my own," she reminded him. "As for the burden you perceive I carry..." The mask slipped, some of the pain and turmoil she was enduring leaking through. "Everything that comes to pass is God's will. That's what I was raised to believe and it is the only solace I have. My husband's suffering is over and for that I must be grateful. Now I must forge on and..." She faltered and he saw his chance:

"Yes, that's right! You have to go on, Patricia. You're still alive, still young. There's no goin' back and no point torturin' yourself about it. What's done is done." But if he'd retained any hope that his words would somehow heal her, bring her back from whatever hell she'd consigned herself, her reaction told him otherwise.

"Oh, *God*..." she wailed, her hands leaping to her face.

"What is it?" He took a step toward her. "There's somethin' else, isn't there?"

The misery and torment she'd been keeping inside could no longer be confined. Her face crumpled, grief erasing her pretty features, gripping and shaking her slight figure so that her next words were almost incomprehensible. "*I am ...carrying his child.*" She held out her hands, palms toward him, as if showing him the stain there. "I was waiting for— for the right moment to tell him. But he was so consumed with jealousy...I couldn't. I was furious, I *hated* him. His drinking and foul accusations...as if I would...I would ever..." He couldn't make out the rest of it. She was sobbing, inconsolable. Consumed by sorrow and guilt, lost and perhaps for all time.

He could do nothing for her. It was not his place to offer comfort. Indeed, it was clear his presence was only making matters worse. There had never been a chance of anything happening between them. He should have realized it all along. He wasn't a suitor, her husband's rival, merely another man selfishly pursuing her, neglecting to take into account *her* feelings and aspirations, the incalculable value she placed on time-honored institutions like marriage and motherhood.

She had sworn an oath of fidelity before God.

And Patricia Waring was a woman of her word.

They reached Livingston late that afternoon. He bade a quick farewell to the others, taking his leave of them as soon as civility permitted. The last he saw of Patricia Waring, Caliban was escorting her into the Albemarle Hotel, supporting her with his good arm. She looked frail and tired but still very, very beautiful.

Then the door swung closed behind them and she was gone.

Essie Montgomery was overjoyed to see him again. His original intention was to stop in for a brief visit and then be on his way, but she was a hard woman to resist.

"Don't be in such a rush," she chided him, leading the way to the kitchen, "I want to hear all about what happened." He cringed at the thought of reliving the events of the past two weeks but knew there was no getting around it. It was not a story he was looking forward to telling. She was cooking up a huge pot of dumplings for her other visitor, who was already seated at the table, a place setting in front of him.

"Scoot over, Fatty," she said, "make room for a hungry hunter who, unlike you, has to *earn* his keep." She sniffed the surrounding air. "He smells like it too..." Seaver grinned, glad to be back, enjoying her humor and bonhomie.

Roscoe Van Dyke winked at him. "Never you mind. That's just her way of sayin' she missed you." She menaced him with a big, wooden spoon but it was just for show.

"You two act like an old married couple," Seaver remarked.

"Don't he wish," Essie laughed. "I've had my fill of men. He's welcome to my good cooking but that's it."

"Be different if we was ten years younger, though," Van Dyke quipped.

"Be different if you were a hundred pounds lighter," she fired back, not missing a beat. "Now quit flapping your gums. Mr. Thornton here was about to tell us all about his latest adventures." She frowned. "Although from the look on his face, I'd say he's had a hard time of it."

"It ain't been easy," he admitted. Then, over the course of the meal and coffee afterward, he recounted the entire story, concluding with the discovery of Philip Waring's mangled body.

"May God have mercy on his soul," she said once he was done, crossing herself.

"So," Van Dyke summed up, "Waring's dead and the cat lives on. Wonder what Foley and his bunch will say to *that*? Last I heard, they're thinkin' of droppin' their bounty idea. The Governor's been gettin' an earful from Washington. Besides, that critter's good for business. Kinda shows Yellowstone is still a wild place. Could be the best thing to happen to this town since President Arthur passed through last year."

It was getting on toward evening before Seaver finally managed to extricate himself. But once he'd escaped Essie's clutches, he found Van Dyke loitering on the front walk, waiting to have a private word with him.

"I got a message to pass along." The lawman followed him over to his horses. "You, uh, ever run into that Seaver fella, be sure to tell him Hec Steubing's been around, inquirin' after him. Had some paper with him, includin' what looked like a valid warrant. Tell him this Steubing's a serious man and that he should watch himself."

"I'll do that. Thanks...on his behalf."

Seaver climbed up onto the Nag. Checked to make sure his pack horse (still unnamed) was well-secured, nodded to Van Dyke and started on his way.

His plans had changed. Montana was a bust but the Great Northwest still beckoned. It was literally a different country up there—once he crossed the border he'd be free and clear, no warrants, no Hec Steubing. He nudged the Nag into a trot and before long Livingston was behind them, relegated to mere memory (and not a very happy one at that).

He was still wearing the Colt Peacemaker, just in case anyone tried to deter him from reaching his final destination. And there was the .44 Henry, should it be required, fully loaded and as deadly as its reputation. He felt rejuvenated, ready for just about anything, and for the first time in a long while at ease with himself, content to let his destiny play out, for good or ill.

The sun was setting off to his left, the western sky ablaze. Still time to put some miles behind him and gain a head start. The track was wide enough for a wagon and clearly marked, frequently lined on both sides by a blend of lodgepole pine and various deciduous trees. The air supporting a vast array of scents, his surroundings saturated in color. He felt his mood improve with every step that took him further and further away from a past he no longer considered his own.

Someone was emerging from the tree line about fifty yards ahead of him, taking up a position in the middle of the road. He kept going until they were about thirty yards apart, then halted the Nag.

"That you, Hec?"

The bounty hunter was tall and rail thin, an unassuming exterior that gave a false impression of gawkiness. It had caused more than one desperado to underestimate him, sometimes with fatal results. His reputation was formidable, and it was said that he was equally adept with rifle and pistol.

"I got paper on you, Seaver," he stated without preamble. "Everything legal and aboveboard."

"I'm sure it is, Hec. You wouldn't come all this way if it wasn't."

"'Preciate your saying so." Steubing had a '73 Winchester propped on his thigh and his eyes never left Seaver, missing nothing.

"Don't suppose I could convince you to step aside. Your paper's from Missouri and it's safe to say I won't be back that way again." A corner of Steubing's mouth rose slightly, the equivalent of a smile coming from him. "I got no quarrel with you is all I'm sayin'."

"That may be," the bounty hunter allowed, "but there's still the matter of that deputy sheriff from St. Joe. Way I hear it, he was only a kid."

"I feel bad about that," Seaver conceded, "but he pulled

on me and I did what comes natural. I never saw a badge until it was over and done with."

"I guess you know the family's got influence. They've taken it hard."

"I'm telling you, there was nothin' I could do about it."

Steubing's mouth twitched again. "Tell it to the jury."

"It might not get that far. If he was as popular as you say, someone down there might decide to take justice into their own hands. Wouldn't be the first time."

"You run that risk." Steubing frowned. "Your reputation don't help you none."

"Ain't no way I'd get a fair shake. Not in Missouri."

"Mebbe, mebbe not." For a moment or two they reflected on their circumstances and what was about to come to pass.

"Guess we should get to it." Seaver untied the pack horse, let the line drop to the ground.

"If you say so." Steubing reached up, adjusting his Stetson to the angle of the sun.

"Before we do, I want you to know somethin'. If this goes my way, you're my last one. I'm done with this business, Hec. Fed up with the killin' and runnin' and watchin' my back in case some yellow-bellied son of a bitch decides he wants to make his reputation. To *hell* with it. All of it."

"I hear you. It ain't no life for a white man. And if it's me, I'll only say it's an honor to be the one that puts you in the ground."

"Fair enough." He looped the reins around his pommel, slid the Henry out of its scabbard. "Good luck to you, Hec."

"See you in hell, Seaver." Saluting him with the classic Winchester. "We'll smoke a big stogie together."

With that, Seaver drove his heels into the Nag, spurring

the animal forward, straight at the onrushing rider. A heartbeat later, the Colt was in his right hand, pointing down the track as he hurtled toward Hec Steubing. No time to think, operating purely by instinct. Not panicking or recoiling when the first bullet tore the hat from his head and the second pulped his left ear.

It was just like the first time. A calmness settling over him, his hand rock steady despite the bullets, the galloping horse beneath him, even the insistent throb and burn where his ear used to be.

Never any doubt or hesitation. Thumbing back the hammer, taking careful aim.

Facing down his old nemesis, Death, yet again, if only for the sake of one last, fleeting chance at a better life.

THE END

Acknowledgements

The Last Hunt is a work of fiction, so I trust historical purists will forgive me if I sometimes refuse to allow mere facts to get in the way of a darn good story.

For the record, Theodore Roosevelt did indeed shoot an enormous grizzly in Montana in 1884...just nowhere near Yellowstone Park. On the other hand, I can also tell you that according to Lee Whittlesey (*see below*), recent research has uncovered the existence of some large, aggressive mountain lions present in Yellowstone during the period in question (early 1880's). How about that...

I'm greatly indebted to a number of people who lent their time and expertise to this literary endeavor. Mistakes in content are mine and mine alone. These folks tried to set me straight with their input and advice. Others listed deserve mention for helping in a variety of ways to facilitate the publication of *The Last Hunt*. My gratitude to one and all:

My wife, Sherron Burns, as always, provided astute editorial assistance and unwavering support; Ken Harman acted as my technical advisor and travel companion to Yellowstone National Park and its environs, performing both roles with admirable facility and restraint.

Thanks, as well, to: Bobby Rockwell and the Rockwell Museum of Western Art; John Fryer and Richard S. Wheeler for their genteel company and conversation. My deepest appreciation to Lee Whittlesey at the Yellowstone Heritage and Research Center in Gardiner, Montana. Lee is a terrific historian and raconteur; he insisted that if I was going to write about Yellowstone, at least *get it right*. Thanks, Lee, for helping me bring such a wondrous region to life.

Bibliography

The Yellowstone Story (Volume 1) by Aubrey L. Haines
(Yellowstone Library and Museum Association; 1977)

*The Great Divide: Travels in the Upper Yellowstone in the
Summer of 1874* by the Earl of Dunraven (University of
Nebraska Press; 1967)

The Gunfighters: The Authentic Wild West by James D.
Horan (Crown Publishers; 1976)

*The Peacemakers (Arms and Adventure in the American
West)* by R.L. Wilson (Random House; 1992)

*Death In Yellowstone: Accidents and Foolhardiness in the
First National Park* by Lee Whittlesey (Roberts Rinehart
Publishers; 1995)

Through the Yellowstone Park on Horseback by George W.
Wingate (O. Judd Co.; 1886)

Tough Trip Through Paradise (1878-79) by Andrew Garcia
(Edited by Bennett H. Stein; University of Idaho Press;
1967)

The Look of the Old West: A Fully Illustrated Guide by
William Foster-Harris (Skyhorse Publishing; 2007)

A Lady's Life in the Rocky Mountains by Isabella L. Bird
(Dover Publications; 2003)

Cliff Burns

Westering Women and the Frontier Experience (1800-1915) by Sandra L. Myres (University of New Mexico Press; 1982)

Seeking Pleasure in the Old West by David Dary (Alfred A. Knopf; 1995)

Men of the West (Life in the American Frontier) by Cathy Luchetti (W.W. Norton; 2004)

The Rise of Theodore Roosevelt by Edmund Morris (Random House; 2010)

The Tiger: A True Story of Vengeance and Survival by John Vaillant (Alfred A. Knopf; 2010)

Cliff Burns has been a professional author for over twenty-five years. His previous books include the supernatural thrillers *So Dark the Night* and *Of the Night*. He resides in western Canada with his wife, Sherron, and two sons, Liam and Samuel.